THE
PAPER TRAIL
MYSTERY

A PIANO TEACHER MYSTERY

Ann Buys

COZY CAT
P R E S S
ISBN: 978-1-952579-18-9
Printed in the United States of America
10 9 8 7 6 5 4 3 2 1

To Mom who, from my childhood on, has accepted my literary offerings with love and enthusiasm.

CHAPTER ONE

The autumn wind had blown fiercely all day, threatening a storm. One hadn't been expected—the wind had only meant to sweep the last of the dry leaves from the trees—but a storm was blowing in all the same.

Maggie Brown awoke with a start, immediately recognizing the shrill blare of the town siren that was signaling the volunteer firemen and paramedics to some emergency. Surprisingly, it wasn't the siren that had awakened her though. She had lived in Trenton for seven years and was well accustomed to its noise by now. It wasn't the wind either. She had never minded its blustery moan as it blew through the cracks of the old house. What had brought her out of a deep sleep was the unmistakable pain she was experiencing.

She waited for the discomfort to pass then sat up and looked at the clock on the bookcase. It was only nine-twenty. She realized she'd fallen asleep on the couch waiting for Hal to get home.

Maggie slowly got up and made her way to the bedroom where the girls were sleeping—six-year old Janie and four-year old Susan. *Thank goodness the siren hadn't woken them,* she thought.

She walked into the kitchen to get a drink of water, hoping the pain was just a fluke, perhaps a bit of false labor, but when it happened again just a few minutes later, she realized it was the real thing. Wishing she'd showered earlier but knowing it was too late to do it now, she put on her coat and quietly left the house.

Another pain came as soon as she got outside. She sat on the top step and bent her head against the wind, waiting for it to pass. Then she hurried down the porch and headed towards the neighbor's house. The baby wasn't supposed to come this early. The doctor had scheduled a caesarian section for two weeks from today, hoping to avoid labor all together, but that was one appointment she knew she wouldn't be keeping. The baby was coming tonight.

"Oh, you poor dear!" Mrs. Bolger exclaimed when she saw Maggie standing on her front step. She summoned her husband away from the television set and gave him short but explicit instructions on how to get Maggie to the hospital as quickly as possible. Then she assured Maggie that she would go next door and watch the girls for her.

"And when Hal gets back," she said, "I'll send him right along too, to the hospital. Don't you worry; it'll all work out!"

Just as the wind had been warning all day, the snow started to come in—not soft and even but in a great rush. It stuck in clumps on the windshield, making it difficult to see. *Thank goodness they lived in a small rural town,* Maggie thought. The road to the hospital wouldn't have much traffic on it this time of night. Still, they might have some trouble staying on it. The snow was making it more slippery with each passing moment.

"It looks like the emergency entrance's blocked by the paramedics," Mr. Bolger stated when they arrived. "If I park close, are you good to walk in or should I bring you a wheelchair?"

"No wheelchair—I'll be fine walking in. Just let me off here."

"Not on your life, or rather, *my* life!" he exclaimed. "Florence would have my neck if I didn't see you through those doors!"

Maggie allowed Mr. Bolger to walk her in. She could tell he wasn't comfortable with the task he'd been given and was relieved when the nurse told him he could go, that she would take it from there. Maggie thanked him for his help then was quickly taken down the hall in a wheelchair.

"I'm Nurse Kelli. We'll get you to a room right away. Then I'll call Dr. Jensen."

When Maggie saw the nurse again, she could tell something was wrong. She was acting as calmly as possible as she prepped Maggie for the C-section, but her previous, easy going nature was gone.

"Is it the doctor?" Maggie asked nervously, thinking the worse. "He's not able to come, is he?"

"No, no… Dr. Jensen's on his way," Nurse Kelli assured Maggie in her best professional voice. "No problems there! It won't be much longer now before that baby of yours makes an entrance!" Her words were encouraging but her face showed something very different.

"Have you seen Hal yet?" Maggie asked. "He should've been here by now. I don't understand what's keeping him."

Nurse Kelli shook her head then tried changing the subject. "Is this your first baby?" she asked.

"No, I've got two girls at home."

"Who's watching them tonight?"

"My neighbor, Mrs. Bolger. You might know her. She works here at the hospital on Wednesdays as a pink lady."

"Oh, yes, I know her. Your girls are in good hands!"

Maggie couldn't agree more but wasn't able to say so just then. Another pain went tearing through her body, temporarily disabling her. The nurse tried to make her as comfortable as possible then left to see if the doctor had come in yet. It wasn't good for a two-time caesarian patient to go into hard labor.

On the next floor down, the emergency room doctor had his hands full. A traffic accident had brought four people in—two with cuts and bruises, one with a broken leg and possible back trauma, and one in critical condition who wasn't expected to last through the night. The front office was trying to locate the relatives of the injured victims but the weather outside was making it almost impossible to do so. Phone lines were down, and roads were being closed as the storm continued to play havoc on the small town.

When the lights went out in Maggie's house, Mrs. Bolger found some matches in the kitchen cabinet and lit the candles on the bookcase in the front room. Then she sat on the couch and waited, watching the candlelight make strange shadows as it flickered on the wall. Her husband Roy should be getting back any minute now—Maggie's husband should too. Florence

Bolger hoped neither of them was stranded in a ditch somewhere from sliding off snow-covered roads.

The storm raged on until the early hours of the morning. When it finally stopped, the city snowplows came out to begin the extensive job of clearing the roads. Up and down the streets they went, helping to make the roads drivable once again.

With the arrival of the sun later that morning, the citizens of Trenton came out too, to shovel their walks and driveways. Children, bundled in warm coats and hats, began the important task of building snowmen in their yards. Sleds were hauled up hills for a slippery ride down and ice skates were dug out of closets to try on the frozen ponds.

The storm had brought the town of Trenton a snowy wonderland to enjoy.

In the hospital, Maggie awakened to the wintry scene just outside her window. For a moment, she thought it had all been a dream, that Mr. Bolger hadn't brought her to the hospital, that she hadn't just had a baby, and that the storm had missed her town altogether. When she realized it wasn't a dream, she began to cry uncontrollably. Her entire life had been changed forever, and all because of a snowstorm.

She'd named the baby Wesley Hal after his father. He had his same blue eyes and light hair, unlike his sisters who had Maggie's dark eyes and wild auburn curls. Maggie usually put braids in Janie's and Susan's hair to keep their locks under control, but today Grandma was in charge.

She brushed their hair out and helped them dress for the services.

"We should plan on some food for afterwards," Maggie's mother had suggested.

"The church ladies are bringing something in."

Maggie's mother had come to help and to give her best advice. "You should move back home when this is all over," she had told her. "You're going to need help with the kids—you can't raise them alone."

There was too much to decide right now. Maggie had been doing her best just to get through the last few days without breaking down mentally and physically. Trying to recover from a C-section was enough for anyone, let alone taking care of a new baby and two children while planning her husband's funeral.

"I'll decide later," she told her mother, "when things settle down enough for me to think."

"I know you need time to think," her mother agreed, "but time is a luxury you don't have.

There are some decisions that have to be made now."

The church house was full. Hal had been a likeable person and had many friends. The receiving line went all the way down the hall and out onto the sidewalk. Flower arrangements, sent by numerous sympathizers, crowded the front of the chapel. Hal's relatives, some whom Maggie had never even met, came through the line, introducing themselves and expressing condolences. Even the paramedics who'd assisted Hal at the accident came to show their support and, of course, his fellow reporters from the *Trenton Daily Reporter* were in attendance as well.

After the graveside service, hordes of people came to the house to lend more support. Casseroles, cakes, rolls and lunch meats had been put out by the church ladies' committee to feed the mourners. Maggie was hugged many times over as she listened patiently to the words of sympathy directed towards her but was secretly wishing all along for everyone to leave.

When the last guest finally did leave, Maggie collapsed on her bed, exhausted. Her mother quietly closed the bedroom door, fed the baby, and got the girls into their nightgowns.

The next morning, Maggie knew she was going to have to confront her mother about wanting to stay in her own house. She was dreading it but knew she couldn't delay it any longer. She also knew how hard it would be to live on her own. Having her mother there to help with the baby and the girls the last week had been a luxury. But, realistically, that would have to come to an end and her mother would need to go back home to her own life, leaving Maggie to deal with hers.

She found her mother in the kitchen, helping the girls choose the cereal they wanted for breakfast. Taking a deep breath, Maggie walked in, ready to tell her what she'd decided.

Suddenly, she froze, unable to move or to make a sound. The town siren had started its high-pitched, blaring noise once again, signaling the firemen and paramedics to a new emergency.

The shrill scream was intruding into her house and waking her baby.

"I'll get him," her mother said as she hurried towards the nursery, but Maggie didn't hear. She was reliving the night of the awful storm, the night she'd lost Hal.

Her mother was soon back, holding the baby and patting him on the back, whispering soft words of comfort. Maggie looked up at her, her whole body shaking. Sadly, she knew she'd have to leave Trenton after all. Her life here was over.

CHAPTER TWO

"Lou-ee-za! It's me... Sofie! Are you home?"

The across-the-street neighbor came bursting through the front door, unannounced and slightly out of breath. "Have you seen Candy Corn? She's missing again!"

Maggie was in the front parlor, teaching a piano lesson to eight-year-old Becky Stiltson.

"Mom's in the kitchen," she said, trying not to show her irritation at being interrupted, once again, by the enigmatic force that was Sofie. "She might know where your cat is."

"Sorry...I didn't mean to interrupt—I keep forgetting about your lessons. It's just that darn cat! I swear she likes this house better than mine! Shall I go through to the kitchen then?" She began waddling down the hall, not waiting for an answer.

Maggie closed Becky's lesson book then walked her out onto the front porch. It was time to end the lesson anyway. Becky's mother would be coming soon to pick her up.

The large oak tree in the front yard had changed from a shady green to a vibrant yellow and the orange flowers of the trumpet vine hung flamboyantly on the trellis along the side of the house.

Autumn was showing its best, here in the small town of Springville.

"There's your mom, and right on time!' Maggie watched the familiar blue station wagon pull into the driveway. "Tell her you passed off the daffodil piece today—she'll be glad to hear it—and don't forget to practice your scales this week!"

Becky waved goodbye then hurried to get in the car so she wouldn't have to promise her teacher something she had no intention of doing.

It had been almost a year since Maggie had moved her family back home to live with her mother. Janie was in the second grade now and Susan had started morning kindergarten.

Wesley was just beginning to walk, his little legs toddling around the house, getting him into everything he could reach. Grandma watched the kids every afternoon while Maggie taught piano lessons in the front parlor to bring in extra money.

The town of Springville hadn't changed much. Maggie had begun her life there in the mid-fifties, started grade school at Springville Elementary in the sixties, and had graduated high school in the early seventies. She had met Hal that first year of college. They'd been married just over a year later and had moved to his beloved hometown of Trenton. Now she was back in Springville, feeling that her life had gone full-circle and way too soon. Wasn't that supposed to happen at the end of your life?

"Grandma says it's time to eat," Janie suddenly announced through the front door screen.

Maggie opened it and went through. "What has Grandma fixed for us tonight?"

"It's green bean casserole," Janie said, pulling a face. "Mommy, I hate green beans! Can I just have a bowl of cereal instead?"

"You don't want to hurt Grandma's feelings, do you? How about just taking a little bit on your plate? That way, after a bite or two, you won't have to eat any more and can fill up on rolls instead. I know you like *them.*"

Maggie's mom had the table all set, as usual, and Janie and Susan hurried to find their places.

Wesley was in his highchair, already eating one of the rolls.

Maggie sat down in the chair beside him. "Did Sofie find her cat?" she asked.

"Yes. Candy Corn had made her way into the kitchen earlier and had been playing with Susan on the rug by the fireplace. She's been there for most of the afternoon. Why, did she interrupt your lessons again?"

Maggie put a spoonful of casserole on Susan's plate. "No, not really. I just don't see why she thinks she can come into our house—*your house*—without knocking first."

"Probably because she's been doing it forever. She's one of my oldest friends, you know, so I really don't mind. I'll remind her again to come to the back door when you're teaching lessons."

Maggie looked across the table at Janie and winked. She had put some of the casserole onto her plate and was trying out a tiny bite. Maggie passed the rolls over to her and smiled.

"Did you notice Clara Wellington at the Sunday services last week, sitting by that nice-looking young man?" Maggie's mother casually asked as she spooned some casserole onto her own plate. "Didn't he have on the nicest suit and tie? He's Clara's son, you know, come down from Chesterfield to visit.

He has a job there as a clerk, working for an accounting service —I can't remember the name of it—but it's a good, solid job. And he's so nice looking, I can't understand why he's not married yet! Did you notice him? We were only two rows behind them." Maggie's mom was obviously hinting at something Maggie knew only too well.

"Yes, I noticed," Maggie decided to play along. "And I've given him a lot of thought this week as well."

"You have!?" Her mother almost jumped out of her seat. "Well, what have you been thinking? That he's good looking? Of course, you'd have noticed that. What else have you thought?" She leaned over the table in anticipation. Could her daughter finally be thinking of dating? After all, plenty of time had passed since her husband had died.

"Actually, I've been wondering how in the world Clara Wellington could have given birth to someone so… how did you put it? Someone so good-looking and well dressed!"

Maggie's mom sat back in her chair and slowly took a bite of the casserole, trying not to smile.

Clara Wellington was, after all, about as homely a woman as she'd ever seen. "She's a good woman though," she said, with a touch of reprimand in her voice. "You shouldn't be so unkind, Maggie."

Maggie apologized. "Yes, she is a good woman—one of the best. But I really don't have any designs on her son. As I've told you before, I don't plan on dating for a long time, if at all."

Her mother shook her head in exasperation at her daughter's obstinate attitude but said nothing more. Janie had started to chatter about her friends at school and Susan was talking on about her favorite subject—Candy Corn. The meal continued without further conversation about nice looking, dateable young men.

When Wesley began to throw the last bits of his dinner onto the floor, Maggie knew he was finished. She took him out of his highchair and wiped his hands and face with her napkin.

"I'm taking him upstairs for his bath," she told her mother. "Will you send the girls up when they're finished? And leave the dishes for me to do! Your television program is on tonight. You don't want to miss it."

Later that night, after getting her children fed and tucked into bed, Maggie sat alone on the back porch, watching the moon as it shone down upon the small town. It had started to get dark early now and the evenings were a bit colder as well. She pulled her jacket around herself tightly, not so much to keep out the cold as to wrap herself up in a feeling of personal security, something that had been sorely lacking since Hal was no longer beside her. Suddenly, she heard the back door open and her mother appeared, interrupting her thoughts.

"Is everything all right?" she asked. "Wesley hasn't woken, has he?"

"No, he's still fast asleep—everything is fine," her mother assured her. "It's just that Mrs. Barker from the community playhouse called again. They still need a pianist for the winter musical."

Maggie smiled. Her mother was persistent if nothing, and obviously ready for round two of suggesting how she should meet other people. And by 'other people,' of course, she meant prospective husbands.

"I'm still not interested," Maggie replied, then before her mother could protest, quickly added, "It's just too soon. I still need a bit more time."

"Phyllis Tinney has moved to West Belview, as you know, and left the community playhouse without an accompanist. It has nothing to do with me wanting you to be involved. I know better than to try! It's just that they're so desperate for someone to come and play the piano for them that they—well, they keep ringing me up. You really should consider doing it."

Maggie frowned. "Okay, I'll think about it. But who would watch the kids when I needed to be gone? I feel I'm already using you too much."

"Rehearsals are every Tuesday and Thursday night, and it would only be for a few months. I wouldn't mind watching the kids a little extra for that bit of time. Besides, they're asleep in their beds by then."

Maggie remembered how good her mother was at arguing a point. She slid over to make room for her on the step then placed an arm around her shoulder. "I promise to think about it," she repeated softly. Her mother was, after all, only trying to help.

"Is everything all right? You seem a bit depressed. You're not coming down with something, are you?"

Maggie took a minute, wondering how to answer. Instead, she asked her mom a question.

"How long did it take, after dad died?"

Her mother smiled. So, this was what was bothering her daughter. "A long time. It took a very long time. You coming to live with me, and those sweet kids of yours, that has helped a lot."

Maggie was surprised. She hadn't thought of her mom still being lonely, not after all these years.

"It wouldn't be normal to get over someone you loved as much as Hal in just a few weeks," her mother reminded her.

"But it's been more than a few weeks—it's been almost a year now!"

"Give it time, Maggie, dear; just give it time. It'll hurt less if you get involved with other people—and no, teaching piano lessons doesn't count! You should seriously re-think the community playhouse!"

They sat in silence for a while. Suddenly, Maggie's mother jumped up all excited. "Just look at those leaves!" she exclaimed, as if she'd just discovered gold under the oak tree. "Why, they're almost covering the lawn!"

"I can rake them for you if they'll wait until Saturday," Maggie volunteered.

"Thanks, but I think I'll give Zachy a call. He'll be more than happy to come over and rake them for me. Maybe, while he's at it, I can talk him into trimming that hedge. Look how it's overgrown!"

And, just like that, Maggie's mother had changed the subject. She was good at that too.

CHAPTER THREE

The director for the Springville Community Playhouse, a Mrs. Trudy Barker, brought the music early Monday morning for Maggie to look over before her first rehearsal.

Maggie invited her into the parlor when she arrived. Mrs. Barker was a highly decorative woman, with lots of colorful scarves tied around her plump shoulders and lots of red lipstick on her ample and very talkative lips. After telling Maggie how much she appreciated her accepting the position with the amateur theater, she went on to gossip about half the town. Maggie was surprised at the extent of her social knowledge. Mrs. Barker knew things and didn't mind telling her all about them.

"Sally and Stephanie Woodford were put in charge, to head the committee to cut down the trees along Main Street. They're sisters, you know. Well, of course, the citizens of Springville weren't about to stand by and watch their precious trees be cut down, and all because of two busybodies! They got together and fought off the Woodfords and the city council as well. It was quite the battle! Concord and Lexington had nothing on the Springville Tree Savers Society!

And, as you can see when you go down Main Street, the trees are still there. However, the Woodford sisters have long since moved to other parts—who knows where."

"Oh, really? I don't think I knew them…"

"And Wilson Wainwright from the auto garage was another strange one, thinking he could fashion a sign from parts of an old John Deere tractor! I can tell you now, it only was up for a week before the wind brought it down. He should've known, you know, that the wind blows straight down that canyon fiercer than anything! Why, no one would ever think of building anything in that wind-blown, no-man's land of a canyon where he lives, especially not a sign made from a John Deere tractor. It was just plain foolishness on his part! But then, Wilson Wainwright was never known for being overly bright if you know what I mean. Good thing no one was hurt, that's all I can say…"

"Yes, good thing."

Maggie patiently listened as her guest talked on, knowing she'd have to run out of people to talk about sooner or later. She was hoping, though, for it to be sooner.

"…it was on the south end of town, in the house by the creek, Maybelle Cunningham had her prize-winning geese all ready to take to the county fair, but as she was loading them all up in her pickup, they got in the creek instead and… well," she stopped momentarily to chuckle over the mud-caked feathers, "it was a pity they had to be disqualified…"

Maggie's mind began to wander. She decided that her occasional, polite comments to the one-sided conversation were really not necessary. Mrs. Barker wasn't listening anyway!

Maggie kept glancing at the clock on the bookcase, watching it move from a half hour, to an hour, then longer as Trudy Barker talked on and on, nonplussed. With each new subject, Maggie heard about people she didn't know and whom she couldn't care less about anyway. She tried scooting to the edge of her chair, hoping Mrs. Barker would take a hint, but she was obviously not to be budged.

"You know, it was the Pence woman—the one who sang the offertory on Sunday—who found him. She has such a lovely voice, don't you think? Well, I can tell you now, she got quite a shock, seeing him like that! Perhaps you knew him? He was the mayor of Trenton. Isn't that where you used to live?"

"What? Trenton, did you say?" Maggie's ears picked up at the mention of her old town.

"Yes, Trenton, my dear," Mrs. Barker repeated, enunciating the words as if Maggie had a hearing impairment. "The *mayor*. Miss Pence found him in the park, sitting on a bench, dead as he could be! They say he had a heart attack or a stroke or something. Really, he was much too young for that sort of thing!"

Maggie couldn't believe what she was hearing. "Mayor Simple? Are you sure it was him? I was acquainted with his wife through the Friends of the Library Committee when I lived there. What she must be going through!"

Mrs. Barker suddenly looked at Maggie with uncharacteristic sympathy on her animated face.

"You, my dear, should know more than anyone what she must be going through, losing you own husband at such an early age!"

She patted Maggie's arm to show her concern then suddenly stood, ready to go. Surprised, Maggie walked her to the door and watched her maneuver herself down the steps. As soon as she was out of sight, Maggie ran back into the house to pick up the phone. She had to hear more about Mayor Simple's untimely death, and if anyone would have the scoop on things from Trenton, it would be her old neighbor, Florence Bolger.

The drive to Trenton seemed longer than the usual thirty minutes. Maggie left early in the morning, just after she got Janie and Susan to school. As usual, her mom had been more than willing to watch Wesley.

The traffic along the interstate was minimal this time of day, so that wasn't the cause of the seemingly lengthy commute. Returning to a town she'd vowed to leave in the past was making her nervous, and that alone was making the trip seem longer than it really was.

Florence Bolger had told Maggie all about the mayor's heart attack over the phone yesterday and about how nice his funeral had been. She'd then gone into details about the funeral—the music and the speakers, and how lovely the flowers were—before she started in on the poor, grieving widow.

"Dolores is simply devastated!" she'd said. "I saw her at the store, just a few days' ago, and she could hardly even speak, she was so overcome with emotion!"

After hearing what Mrs. Bolger had to say about Dolores Simple, Maggie decided then and there that she needed to go back, just for a day, to Hal's hometown. She would stop by Dolores's house and give her a plate of homemade cookies and tell her how sorry she was for her loss. It wouldn't take long, but it was something she needed to do.

She parked in the familiar circular driveway when she arrived then walked up the porch and rang the bell. The Simple's front yard, usually so neat and cared for, looked forgotten. The hedge along the side needed trimming and the lawn looked like it hadn't seen a mower in weeks.

A dog began to bark on the other side of the fence, announcing Maggie's arrival. Soon, the door opened. Dolores Simple, still in her pajamas and robe, reluctantly asked her in.

"These are for you." Maggie handed her the plate of cookies. "I heard what had happened, about your husband, that is—from my old neighbor, Florence Bolger. Well, I wanted to come and see you and tell you how sorry I am." Maggie knew her words sounded a bit lame. "I hope this isn't a bad time."

"Thank you," Dolores said, forcing a smile at her guest. She took the plate of cookies from her then turned and went into the kitchen, leaving Maggie conspicuously alone in the foyer. Maggie waited, hesitant to sit down without first being asked. She looked around the room, noticing the thick dust on the tops of the bookcase and coffee table. This wasn't like Dolores at all, not to keep her home immaculately clean.

When she finally came back into the room, Dolores made some excuse about why she'd left Maggie alone for so long. "The phone, you see—everyone keeps calling. Please, would you like to sit down?" Her voice sounded strained.

"I won't stay long," Maggie said, moving a fringed pillow out of the way before sitting on the flower-printed sofa. "I just want to let you know how very sorry I am. When I heard the news... well, it was hard to believe."

Dolores managed a smile. "And you came all this way to tell me? That is very nice of you."

Maggie felt very uneasy and was beginning to wish she hadn't come at all. Dolores was obviously not in any mood for visitors.

"Well, I probably shouldn't stay—you must have a million things you need to be doing and I *did* just drop in without letting you know I was coming." She stood, ready to leave.

"You can't go already! You just got here!" Dolores's mood suddenly changed. "Please, sit back down! We have a lot to catch up on."

"Well, perhaps just for a minute. I really should've called ahead and let you know I was coming."

"No, no," Dolores protested. "I'm glad you dropped in. We need to visit—to talk about things we've been doing, you know —catch up. Heaven knows it's been much too long since we've talked! And the cookies! How nice of you to bring them for me. Did you make them yourself?"

Dolores had become very talkative. It was like she'd just come out of a daze and had noticed, for the first time, that she had a guest in her living room.

"What have you been doing with yourself since you moved away?" she asked, animatedly. "I heard you moved in with your mother in Springville. Do you have a job there?"

"Well, I'm teaching piano lessons. And I'm playing for the community playhouse. Starting to, anyway. My first rehearsal is tonight."

"I'm so glad to hear you're keeping yourself busy. I used to do a bit of community acting myself a few years' back. It's great for getting out and meeting other people."

"So, I've heard." Maggie thought briefly of her mother.

Dolores shifted in her seat. She picked up one of the sofa cushions and nervously began to fluff it. "You must remind me why you moved away in the first place," she asked.

All at once, the reason Maggie had moved away came back to her. Temporarily frozen, she dropped the pillow she'd been holding then immediately began to apologize.

"I'm… I'm so sorry—I didn't mean to be so insensitive. In my excitement to see you, I'd forgotten about the accident—about Hal," she blurted out.

"Don't worry about it," Maggie said, trying to put her at ease. "You've had a lot on your mind lately—you shouldn't be expected to remember about Hal."

"Yes. You know exactly what I'm going through, don't you? Greg and Hal—both dead and buried."

She looked at Maggie and her face filled with grief. Suddenly, and without warning, Dolores began to sob uncontrollably, making it impossible for her to speak. Maggie handed her a tissue from her purse and waited patiently for her to stop.

"Something's wrong, you see," Dolores said, trying to gain control of herself. She wiped her nose on the tissue and dried her eyes. "Greg shouldn't have died. I don't believe it was a heart attack."

Maggie was surprised and confused at the statement Dolores had just made. "What do you mean?" she asked. "Surely, the doctors would've said something if they thought Greg's death was something besides a heart attack."

"He was just too young and never had any heart problems before. Someone wanted him to die, you see." Dolores looked around the room fearfully, as if she was going to be the next victim of an imaginary crime. "Someone—*murdered* him, I know it!"

The sobbing started all over again, but not out of grief this time. Dolores was genuinely frightened.

Maggie tried to calm her down, knowing nerves were getting the better of her. She remembered her own frazzled nerves after Hal's death. Only time would make them fade, and Dolores's were still fresh, making her believe things that weren't real.

"I… I've got an appointment soon and really should be getting ready now, so if you don't mind…" Dolores's sobbing ended as abruptly as it had begun, and she was now telling Maggie it was time for her to leave. "You will come again, won't you? Perhaps tomorrow? We still have a lot to catch up on."

Maggie was caught off guard by the request. "Well, I can't come tomorrow," she said, then seeing the disappointment on Dolores's face added, "but, perhaps another day?"

Dolores forced a smile then walked Maggie to the door. Suddenly, she took hold of her arm and in a low voice, as if she expected someone to be eavesdropping, whispered, *"The papers are in the broom closet. Somebody should know, just in case anything happens to me."*

Maggie looked at her, surprised and a little afraid herself. "What papers? What are you talking about?"

But Dolores didn't answer. She hurried away, down the hall and into her room, shutting the door behind her.

Maggie immediately wondered if she had acted this strangely when Hal had died. She couldn't decide whether to be afraid of Dolores or sympathetic. She hurried out of the house and into her car, sorry she'd ever come in the first place, then headed back to Springville where life was safe and normal.

CHAPTER FOUR

That night, after getting the kids to bed, Maggie walked the two blocks to the community playhouse. It was in an old, renovated barn—something that the townspeople had built after many years of fundraisers and contributions.

She walked through the dry leaves that covered the sidewalk, thinking about what Dolores had said earlier that day. Could someone really have murdered Mayor Simple? Things like that just didn't happen in Trenton. Why, the three policemen who patrolled the town probably hadn't even seen a jaywalker in years.

Turning the corner, Maggie stopped for a moment to take in her surroundings. Nothing much had changed here in Springville. There, in the park, was where Hal had proposed. It had been a bright summer day and the two of them had just had a picnic under the tall oak tree—sandwiches and a chocolate cake that she'd made just for the occasion. She even remembered what she'd worn. It was a light peach-colored blouse with little white pearl buttons up the front, and cut-off jeans. Hal had worn a white cotton shirt, open at the neck, with his sleeves rolled up just below the elbows. It had been a warm but pleasant day and she'd been very happy, sitting there with Hal. But now, the cold air was creeping around her, reminding her that the summer day of long ago was just a distant memory.

Maggie pulled her coat tight about her then hurried on towards the old barn. She'd always admired the impressive-looking building that now hosted the local theatre. The renovation had kept the original red of the barn and had added some white lattice work at the entrance. A tastefully done sign was hung by the double doors that served as the entrance. *Springville Theatre* was printed in big, bold letters, welcoming all to come inside.

Inside, the first thing that greeted her was a concession stand. Popcorn, drinks, and assorted wrapped candies were offered to patrons at double the price to help finance the running of the theatre. Past the concessions, a double door led into the main theatre. Terraced seating rose upwards in eight rows along each of the four walls surrounding the stage, making the perfect setting for a 'theatre in the round'. Long curtains hung from the rafters just behind the seating, not only as décor but also to create a walkway for actors and stage crews for behind the scenes maneuvers.

Maggie was surprised to see the theatre was all but deserted when she arrived. No one was there, except herself and one old man who was hammering some nails into a set in the corner of the barn. He looked up briefly as Maggie walked towards him.

"If yer one of them actors," he informed her, "then yer a bit early, you know. The others won't be coming in fer another—oh, I suspect a half an hour or so."

"No, I'm not an actress. I'm Maggie Brown, the new accompanist," she said, introducing herself. "I came a bit early so I could try out the piano before the others arrived."

"Well, it's right over there—the piano, that is." He pointed to the opposite corner. "They keep it there during rehearsal, but it's moved behind the curtain next to the lobby entrance when the play begins. That's when the drummer and those other instruments are added."

Maggie thanked him and asked his name.

"I'm Benson. I come in to help with the sets—have been doing it fer years." He tilted his head, looking critically at the work he'd done, then picked up another nail to resume his hammering.

Maggie walked over to the piano and sat down on the wobbly bench, thinking the piano had seen better days. She tried a few chords up and down the keyboard. *Well, the old thing might look a wreck,* she thought, *but it had what it takes!* It had a good touch, although a bit loose, and a bright tone—perfect for the cavernous old barn. She opened her music and started to practice.

Halfway through the score, she heard someone enter the theatre and then a man's voice singing along with her accompaniment. She glanced up to get a good look at him. Immediately, the thought went through her mind that this was someone her mother would approve of. He was nice looking, probably in his mid-thirties, had short, sandy-colored hair, and could sing well—everything her mother looked for when she was trying to line her daughter up with a prospective husband.

"You must be our new accompanist," he said, holding out his hand for her to shake. "I'm Rob Stanger, and you're Maggie Brown? We've needed you badly—and for quite some time now. Mrs. Barker has been plunking out one-finger melodies on the piano, trying to rehearse us on our parts."

Before Maggie could say anything, Mrs. Barker suddenly appeared as if on cue. "And doing a pretty good job of it too, even if I do say so myself. Hi, Maggie. Good to have you here."

Others were now pouring in through the lobby and onto the stage. Mrs. Barker was giving out instructions as they did, directing them to their places before they could get too chatty with one another.

"Our time is short, people! I want Scene Two, first act, on stage now! Let's go from the top of page twelve."

Scene Two actors hurried onto the stage as everyone else found a seat in the audience to watch.

"Well, I guess this means goodbye," Rob Stanger said to Maggie as he hurried onto the stage.

Maggie quickly found her place for Scene Two in the music then eagerly waited for her cue to start playing.

"Bob Cratchit?!" Mrs. Barker bellowed the name into the crowd seated in the audience.

"Where's my Bob Cratchit?!"

"Here I am!"

A thin man with sharp features and a long nose came running through the lobby door, out of breath.

"You're late, Mr. Milchin!"

The timid man nervously hurried onto the stage and quickly got into place.

"We're at the top of page twelve!" Mrs. Barker repeated.

Mr. Milchin clumsily opened his script book and began reciting his lines.

"… boiled with his own pudding with a stake of holly through his heart…"

"No, no! You've got the wrong lines! Those are for Scrooge!" Mrs. Barker shouted at him.

"Turn the page!"

Mr. Milchin looked appropriately sheepish. "Oh, sorry… sorry. Page twelve, did you say? Okay, I'm ready now."

A half hour later, Maggie was still waiting for her cue to start playing. Mrs. Barker kept running the dialogue for Mr. Milchin again and again, hoping to get him to say it just right. *Poor Mr. Milchin,* Maggie thought. He kept wiping his brow with his handkerchief even though it was quite cool in the old barn. She decided that Mrs. Barker had chosen him for his resemblance to the Bob Cratchit character and not for his acting abilities.

Mrs. Barker finally decided to move onto Scene Three, which took at least another half an hour to block. Maggie was starting to wonder why she'd ever come tonight. They hadn't rehearsed a single song and she was getting tired of sitting on the hard, wobbly old bench.

Some of the other actors and actresses, waiting for their parts to come, began to wander off the set, talking and laughing among themselves. A few of them made their way over to the piano to talk with Maggie. Mrs. Barker made a big deal of shushing them when they got too loud.

"I need quiet here, people!" she would bellow, then continue to work with the characters on stage. Nobody seemed too bothered about her shouting. It was obviously something they were used to.

Maggie started to chat with the group who'd come over to the piano. A woman who looked to be about her own age began introducing everyone.

"And this is Candace; she plays Mrs. Cratchit, and Melanie over there is the spirit of Christmas past and, let's see—the Cratchit children are all seated together, across the room. They are actually brothers and sisters themselves! And there's their mom seated next to them—she's here at every rehearsal, making sure they don't get into any trouble. Oh, and I'm Francis Grayson. I play the young wife of Scrooge's nephew Fred. It's not a big part, but I'm having fun just being here!"

Maggie smiled, glad to be included in this cast of vibrant individuals who, unlike herself, seemed to be having fun.

"I need everyone on stage—*now!*" Mrs. Barker suddenly announced when she realized the second hour of practice was upon them. "Hurry, people! Our time here is short! We need to block the Christmas dance in the Fezziwig scene!"

The entire cast immediately hurried onto the stage, glad to finally be doing something. Without hesitation, Mrs. Barker paired them up into dancing partners.

"Now, make two lines and face your partner, like you would in a Virginia Reel."

Maggie turned to the Fezziwig Dance in her score then waited as Mrs. Barker, once again, proceeded to work on the blocking first. It was interesting, watching the workings of a play, but she had to admit to herself, this wasn't at all what she'd been expecting.

"Kind of boring, isn't it?" Rob Stanger was suddenly at the piano again. "I'll bet you hadn't planned on it being like this. Am I right?"

Maggie smiled. He knew exactly what she was thinking.

"It gets better after a while. Running lines and blocking characters is the tedious part of any rehearsal," he added, trying to make her feel better.

"So, why aren't you on stage now? It looks to me like everyone is needed for the dance."

"Everyone but Scrooge."

"Ah, and that's who you play?"

"Of course, who else would I play?"

Oh yes, the star or nothing for Rob Stanger, Maggie thought to herself, smiling.

"And six, seven, eight... wait!" Mrs. Barker had turned away from the dancers and was looking directly at Maggie now, shouting, "Where is the music? I need the music for the dance!"

"I think she's ready for you to play," Rob informed a very flustered Maggie who quickly found her place in the music and began the introduction. She knew, from the night's observation, that this was just the way things were during rehearsal. Still, she bristled at being shouted at and couldn't help but wonder what she'd gotten herself into.

When play practice was over, Rob walked Maggie out into the cold October night. The leaves from the tops of the trees floated leisurely down and around them, their silhouettes catching briefly in the light from the barn.

"Now, that's a pretty sight, don't you think?" Rob said.

"Yes, autumn does have its moments," Maggie replied as she hurried on ahead. "See you in a few days, at the next practice."

"Wait! Can't I walk you home?" he shouted after her, surprised at her haste to get away.

Maggie wasn't sure she liked where this was going. "Thanks, anyway, but I'll be fine."

"What if you lose your way?"

Maggie stopped, then turned to look at him. "There's no chance of that happening," she informed him. "I grew up in this town, you see. Even after the years I spent in Trenton, nothing has changed since I came back. Trust me, I'll be fine."

"So, you lived in Trenton?" Rob wasn't about to give up so easily. "I've heard there's been a lot happening there lately. In fact, on the five o'clock news, just tonight, they reported an accident on the bridge just outside of town."

"What kind of accident?" Maggie was suddenly interested.

"Well, there's been a lot of controversy over this last election, and when their newly elected mayor suddenly died of a heart attack…"

"Yes, I heard about that…"

"…then this car accident—it was pretty awful—the car slipped off the bridge, right into the Cotton Ridge River! You know, those overpasses can get so icy this time of the year! It's the cold air coming up from underneath them that makes them that way. If there's any water at all—from snow or from rain—well, you can bet it will freeze over, making for a slippery ride and…"

"Yes," Maggie interrupted again. At this rate, she might as well go home and watch the ten o'clock news herself to find out what had happened. "*Who* was it that drove off the bridge?"

"That was why this accident was so sensational," Rob tried to explain. "The police are thinking it could have easily been a suicide and not an accident at all, with her husband dying just a week before. They said she'd been under a lot of strain lately."

"*Who* had been under a lot of strain? Rob, you haven't told me yet who it was that drove off the bridge!"

Rob gave a short laugh. "I guess I haven't! It was the mayor's wife, Dolores Simple. Did you know her?"

The color suddenly drained from Maggie's face. Rob looked at her, realizing he'd just upset her. "I'm sorry," he said. "You probably *did* know her, and here I am, blurting it out like this."

Maggie's thoughts were going a mile a minute as she remembered her visit with Dolores and the strange words she'd spoken. *The papers are in the broom closet...in case anything happens to me.*

"Yes, I knew her," she said, shuddering involuntarily.

CHAPTER FIVE

For the second time that week, Maggie made her way back to Trenton. She reluctantly pulled her car into the circular driveway and stepped out. *Well, here I go,* she thought, ready to play out a scene she'd written in her head but hadn't had time to rehearse. She knew she was going to need all her wits about her this morning.

During the drive there, she'd gone over every possible scenario, trying to figure out the best way to get into Dolores's house and inside her broom closet to find the papers that Dolor had told her about. Maggie knew there was a good chance those papers might not even exist. Yesterday, Dolores had been almost out of her mind with grief over the passing of her husband. She could have easily invented the whole thing, but still, Maggie felt she had to make sure. She owed Dolores that much.

There was another car parked in the driveway, a very expensive looking blue Audi. Maggie remembered Dolores talking about her rich brother at a library committee meeting years ago. At times, she would go on and on, boring everyone to death, bragging about the places he'd go and the things he'd buy for her. Maggie knew there was a very good chance the blue Audi belonged to him.

She opened the trunk of her car and pulled out a box of cleaning supplies—hopefully, her free ticket into Dolores's house—then proceeded up the steps to ring the bell. The door quickly opened. Standing before her was a tall, well-dressed man.

"Yes?"

The man holding the door seemed impatient, as if he he'd just been interrupted from doing something important. He peered out at the slender young woman standing before him who was wearing blue jeans, sneakers, and a bandana in her curly red hair, and asked her what she wanted. The box she was holding, he noticed, was almost as big as she was.

Maggie improvised. "I'm here to do the weekly cleaning. Is Mrs. Simple here?"

The man stared down at her, making her feel very uncomfortable. He briefly told her the sad news—that Dolores had just died in an unfortunate accident. He made the statement without emotion, as if he were the butler announcing dinner was being served.

"So, as you can see, your services aren't needed today or anymore for that matter." With that, he proceeded to close the door on Maggie.

"I'm so sorry to hear about Dolores," Maggie quickly said, holding her position, "but, who are you? Dolores mentioned having a brother—is that who you are?"

"Yes, I'm her brother, Brad Bennington—not that it's any of your business. Now, thank you for coming but…"

"It's already paid for— the cleaning," Maggie said, hoping he'd reconsider if money was involved. "I could just do a bit of dusting and vacuuming then be out of your way in no time at all. I know you must be busy, so I promise I won't be in your way in the least!"

Mr. Bennington took a moment to think it through then decided to let Maggie and her box in.

"The house does need a good dusting," he said. "A realtor will be coming in a few days to list it, and it wouldn't hurt to have it looking its best. Might even bring the price up a bit."

"Yes, appearance is important," Maggie agreed.

Before she could say anything more, Brad Bennington disappeared into a room just off the foyer. Maggie quickly glanced inside before he shut the door. Loose papers were lying haphazardly in the room—some on the desk, others on shelves, some had even fallen upon the lush beige carpeting by the entrance. Brad Bennington seemed to be searching through them in a very rushed, untidy way. Maggie hoped they weren't the papers she was looking for.

She hurried through the front room and into the kitchen, not at all sure where to look for the broom closet. After setting the box of cleaning supplies on the kitchen floor, she took out her first prop, a feather duster. Playing the part of the maid, Maggie made her way through each dusty piece of furniture in the house in search of the mystery room.

It wasn't long before the entire house was free of dust, but still no broom closet had been found. Could Dolores's house have a basement? *That would be a good place for a broom closet,* Maggie thought. She soon found another door just outside the kitchen in the small space that led to the garage.

Good, she thought, *this must be it!* She opened the door to find a narrow wooden staircase that appeared to lead to a basement below. It was so dark, she couldn't be sure, so she carefully made her way down the rickety wooden steps, looking for a light switch as she did. There, at the bottom, next to a water heater, she found what she was looking for. She clicked it on.

The single lightbulb that hung from the ceiling barely illuminated the area, but it was enough for Maggie to see that she was standing in a small cellar. She immediately felt a wave of claustrophobia come over her. She took a deep breath and began to look around.

Just behind the stairs she saw another smaller room. She hurried over to it, wishing she'd brought a flashlight. It was even darker in here. Maggie waited for her eyes to adjust then began to explore. Two rickety wooden shelves stood against its walls, holding a variety of cleaning products, a couple of buckets, and some broken tools. Certain that this was the broom closet Dolores had told her about, she began to look around. As far as she could see, there were no papers in here. Reaching her hand up to feel around at the top, she suddenly let out an involuntary scream. Her fingers had just touched something disgusting. She shuddered when she saw the form of a dead cockroach, laying belly up between the dirty cans.

Suddenly, a wave of reality came over her. What in the world was she doing? *This isn't at all like me*, she thought. The ruse she'd invented about being Dolores's maid and the earnestness with which she'd approached it suddenly began to fade in the face of reality. Of course, Dolores had made the whole thing up! She had let her nerves get the better of her and that was why she was dead now, not because of some mysterious papers hidden in a broom closet!

"What are you doing down here!?"

Dolores's brother had unexpectedly appeared in the doorway and was looking at Maggie suspiciously. "I've been looking all over the house for you!"

Startled, Maggie's heart began to pound. Without thinking, she grabbed an old can from off the shelf. Seeing the word 'wax' written at the top, she said the first thing that popped into her mind.

"The floor in the kitchen—it looked like it needed a bit of polishing, so I came down to get this."

"What happened? I thought I heard you scream."

Maggie forced a laugh. "It was just a cockroach—there, on the shelf. I'm not too…partial to them." she stuttered out the words. "It surprised me; that's all. I didn't mean to upset you."

"That's car wax you're holding there, you know. The floor wax is on the next shelf up." Mr. Bennington pointed to a white and brown container marked 'Quick Shine' that was sitting prominently on the shelf above.

Flustered, Maggie put the can she was holding back in its place and reached for the floor wax instead.

"Will you lock up behind you when you're through waxing the floor?" Brad Bennington asked. "I've got to be leaving."

"Certainly. No problem at all."

He stared at her for a minute longer, as if he wasn't sure about leaving her alone in the house, then turned abruptly and walked up the stairs. Maggie listened until she could no longer hear his footsteps above then decided it was time for her to leave also. This whole thing had turned out to be nothing more than a wild goose chase. Why she'd come, she would never know.

Reaching out to replace the wax on the top shelf, Maggie's hand brushed by what felt to be the cover of a folder. Immediately, her heart started pounding again. Could this be what she'd been looking for? Standing on tiptoes, she grabbed hold of it at the corner.

The dusty folder fell from its shelf before Maggie could stop it. Papers flew everywhere, cascading down upon the cement floor in a confusion of white. Maggie quickly gathered them up. On the cover page, the heading *Minutes of the Westside Hospital Committee Meeting – June 8, 1941* was written in bold letters across the top.

Maggie was confused. *Why would Dolores be hiding minutes to a meeting held over forty years ago?* She hesitated for a moment, wondering if she should take them or not. They must mean something, or why else would Dolores have been so intent on telling her about them?

Without hesitation, Maggie hurried up the stairs, tucked the folder inside her box of cleaning supplies, then quickly left the house before she could change her mind. After all, she rationalized, who would miss a bunch of old papers from 1941?

CHAPTER SIX

A brisk wind came blowing through the city of Springville later that week, leaving a carpet of leaves on the lawn outside. Maggie's mother decided she could wait no longer. It was time to give Zachy a call to come and rake them before the winter snows came.

Janie and Susan watched through the kitchen window as Zachy made pile after pile of the colorful leaves in the backyard.

"Can we go help him?" Janie asked.

Grandma was at the stove, pouring pancake batter into a large frying pan. It was Saturday morning and the family was in the kitchen, waiting for the big breakfast Grandma was making.

"Why don't you go out and ask Zachy if he wants to come in and eat with us?" Grandma said, turning her answer into another question in her usual way. Janie hurried out the back door, excited to tell Zachy about the invite.

Zachy was a tall, lanky thirteen-year old who lived in the neighborhood a few houses down. He was always coming over to help Maggie's mom with things around the house.

Maggie added another place for him at the table. Soon, Zachy was hurrying through the back door, excited at being invited in. He hung his coat on the rack by the door then sat down in his usual chair.

Sitting in his highchair, Wesley began chattering in his baby voice, excited to have someone come new there, but Susan hid behind her mother, too shy to speak.

"How do you like your eggs?" Grandma asked.

"No eggs—thanks anyway—but a few pancakes will be great!" Zachy said, enthusiastically. "I've already had a couple of my mom's omelets before coming over."

Maggie looked up from the table just in time to see her mother's expression. Yes, there it was, the 'I can't believe you just said that' look, followed by the 'oh, well' smile, and thought of the many times she'd seen that same look from her mom when she was growing up.

After breakfast was over, Maggie's girls got their coats on and went outside to play in the leaves. She watched them through the kitchen window as they jumped into the neat piles Zachy had made. He didn't seem to mind—he'd spread a large net on the ground, making it easy to pull the leaves back into another pile so they could jump as many times as they wanted.

"So, are you going to tell me what's been bothering you these past few days?" Maggie's mom asked as she put away the dishes.

"Why do you think something's been bothering me?"

"To start with, your absent-mindedness. Something's on your mind and I'm guessing it has to do with your trip to Trenton last Wednesday."

Maggie wasn't surprised her mother had noticed. As usual, nothing got past her. As briefly as possible, she explained all about Dolores and the strange words she'd said about papers in her broom closet. Quickly, Maggie ran upstairs to retrieve the blue folder, bringing it down for her mother to see.

"And this is what I found, there in Dolores's basement—the minutes of a hospital committee meeting, of all things!" Maggie was starting to feel foolish all over again. "I don't know why I took them—it was all so, impulsive!"

Her mother smiled at her. "You mean, you went to Trenton to find these papers? I'm impressed!"

Maggie couldn't tell whether her mother was really impressed or was just making fun of her.

"Well, it was all for nothing in the end. I've looked over these papers many times and, for the life of me, can't see what Dolores was all worked up about. The minutes show how the committee—six people listed here as being in attendance—had discussed plans for a new hospital. They were also making suggestions on fundraisers. I can't see anything at all suspicious about that."

"And yet, you took the folder with you," her mother noted. "You must've thought it meant something or you wouldn't have taken it."

"But, what can it mean? It's just some boring minutes from a forty-year old meeting!"

"Is there any mention of *money*?" Maggie's mom said the last word as if it had significance.

"What do you mean?"

"Always follow the money, dear, if you're looking to find a crime that's been committed. And, it seems to me that Dolores thought one had. She thought her husband had been murdered, right?"

"Well, yes," Maggie answered, a bit reluctantly. "But her nerves were so shattered, she must have been delirious with grief. I really think that's all there was to it."

"But if there's more, if Dolores was right and if someone *did* murder her husband, and possibly her also, you can bet there was money involved somewhere. Let's look at those minutes again."

Maggie reluctantly opened the folder. "There's a fund raiser here, as I mentioned before. They collected one hundred fourteen dollars and fifty-seven cents for the sale of Christmas wrapping paper."

"Not enough for a murder," her mother stated. "Look again."

"How about this... they discuss here about getting private funding from some of the wealthy individuals in the community. They appointed a Mrs. Thelma Greeley to spearhead it. Maybe they did collect a lot of money privately, but we don't know if what they collected was enough for a murder, do we?"

Her mom smiled as she shook her head. "But we could find out if we did a bit of our own investigating, couldn't we?"

Maggie was surprised. This was a side of her mother she'd never seen before. But then, she'd always been an avid reader of mystery novels. Perhaps she wanted to solve one on her own.

"So, you think these minutes have something to tell us, after all? That we should unravel its mystery?" Maggie humored her, wondering if her mother was serious or not. "What do we do next then?"

"We should look for things that are common."

Her mother quickly moved to her desk for a notepad and pencil. "Let's write everything down. For starters, Dolores telling you about the papers." She looked up from her writing briefly to see her daughter's expression. Yes, there it was, the 'I can't believe my mom is doing this' look. "And don't look at me that way!" she exclaimed. "If we find out there's really nothing to all this, well, we can say we've had a bit of fun along the way!"

Maggie's mother carefully numbered each item in her notepad. The mayor's death, Dolores's death that followed, the hospital minutes, and the money collected for the hospital. "Can you think of anything we need to add?" she asked Maggie.

"Really, mother, this is all too silly! None of those things seem to have anything in common—except for the fact that Dolores and the mayor were husband and wife."

"Then we must add that to the list until we find other similarities."

"And, just *how* are we going to do that?"

"Now, Maggie, stop being critical! The first thing, obviously, is to attend Dolores's funeral. Miss Marple always attended funerals for clues. Maybe you can find out something there."

Maggie let out a long sigh. Leave it to her mother to use an Agatha Christie reference. "And, if we don't find anything…?"

"Then, like I said before, we've had a bit of fun along the way!"

"I'll stop being critical if you'll admit one thing," Maggie said, still unconvinced.

"And, what's that, dear?"

"A funeral isn't exactly the place to have a bit of fun."

CHAPTER SEVEN

Miss Coralee Simple had been married before, years ago, but had dropped the 'Mrs.' when it had all ended just two days' later. After finding her new husband had misrepresented himself in the money department—he was all but broke and instead of owning the yacht they'd been sailing around in, had just borrowed it from a friend—she had demanded a quick annulment and began to pursue her ex-husband's friend—the one who *did* own the yacht. But that had ended in yet another disappointment as well, adding to the long list of things that never seemed to work for Coralee Simple.

Resenting the fact that she had to travel to Trenton today for her sister-in-law's funeral—the second one this month, (her own brother being the first)—she nevertheless knew it would be beneficial to be there. It would give her the opportunity to stop by her deceased brother's house and look for the papers he'd told her about before his sudden and unexpected death.

Using the house key he'd given her years ago when she'd come to stay to get over yet another failed romance, Coralee let herself in. Losing no time at all, she opened the door to Greg's study.

The room was empty! It had all been cleaned out and vacated! And the large mahogany desk—the one that her brother had inherited from their father, was gone! She quickly went through the entire house, trying to find what she'd come for—the rest of Dolores's furniture—all the tacky pieces her sister-in-law had so painstakingly arranged to fit in her outmoded middle-class home—they were still there, but the desk was nowhere in sight.

Coralee's mind immediately leapt to the brother. Yes, Dolores had a brother! He must have taken the desk!

Fuming, she closed the door and left the house. Certainly, Dolores's brother would be at the funeral. She'd find him there and approach him after the services were over. She needed to talk to him about that desk. There was no way she was going to let an outsider take her father's desk away from her! Besides, there was a good chance that the papers were there, hidden inside one of the drawers.

She left the house, carefully locking the door behind her. Now, to remember where the church was. As she drove her car out of the driveway, the thought crossed her mind that it wouldn't be too hard to find, not in this backward, insignificant little town. Why, she could probably drive across the whole town in less than ten minutes, which was exactly how much time she had left before the service began.

Maggie walked into the small kitchen, a bit unsure of herself, but smiling nevertheless at all the familiar faces. "Hi, everyone! It's nice to see you!"

She'd decided to take her mother's advice and attend Dolores Simple's funeral. Afterwards, she could help the church ladies prepare the luncheon while family and friends were at the graveside. Besides, Maggie knew from experience that the small kitchen behind the chapel was the perfect place to hear local gossip.

"Why, it's Maggie Brown!" Selma Wright, the usual spokesman for the group, exclaimed.

"We haven't seen you for—well, what's it been? Almost a year now? Where have you been all this time?"

"I've been living in Springville with my mother. I grew up there, you know."

"Well, it's good to see you back in Trenton, even if it is for a sad occasion. Dolores was such a sweet lady. We all agree, she'll be greatly missed in our community. But it's so nice that you could come!" Selma's enthusiastic welcome was unanimously echoed by all.

"It was a nice funeral, as funerals go," Sally Henderson remarked. "Dolores would've been pleased with it if she could've been there."

"I think, Sally, that Dolores *was* there," Mrs. Carter pointed out. "In fact, I'm certain she was in attendance. Wasn't she the one lying in the coffin?"

A few chuckles went through the group, but most of the ladies remained silent, knowing how inappropriate it was to make jokes at a funeral.

"I didn't mean it that way!" Sally Henderson placed a sandwich on the tray then put her hands on her hips and turned to look at Mrs. Carter. "You know what I meant!"

"All I can say is, it's been such a shock to everyone— Dolores dying, and just a week after her husband!"

"What will happen to their house?" Mrs. Riley, wearing a new paisley-print dress, asked curiously.

"They never had any children, you know. But I think Dolores has a brother. Judith, did she have a brother?" Mrs. Carter asked the small woman next to her who was stirring mayonnaise into a bowl of diced, hard boiled eggs.

"Yes, she does," Judith said. "He was the one seated in the front of the chapel, next to the casket. I hear he's very rich. He took care of all the funeral arrangements."

"What did you think of the coffin he chose? Very *modest*, I'd say," Mrs. Riley emphasized the word 'modest', making Maggie wonder if she was implying that Dolores's brother had been cheap.

"Yes, it was modest," Maryanne Iverson agreed, "but very beautiful too, don't you think?"

Maggie smiled. Maryanne hadn't changed at all. She was the one who was always saying something nice, whatever the occasion.

"I guess it was beautiful, but I really couldn't say for sure. The spray of flowers across the top made it almost impossible to get a good look at it!" Mrs. Riley seemed bent on making her point. "You'd think, with as rich as he is, he'd have sprung for the deluxe model."

"For that matter, you'd think he'd want to pay for the luncheon to be catered instead of having us do it all for free," Selma boldly expressed the words out loud.

"Now Selma. You know we do this for the blessings!" Maryanne sweetly announced.

"Besides, he'd have needed the church hall, so we would've been called in to do exactly what we're doing now anyway."

"Yes, I suppose you're right. But it would be nice to get paid for a change!"

Some of the ladies laughed at Selma's comment, others shook their heads at her outspokenness.

"Did any of you see that stern looking man sitting in the back, right next to the door?" Judith asked, changing the subject. "He was wearing a black hat."

"Yes, I saw him," Mrs. Riley spoke. "He looked like—well, a *crow*, if you know what I mean."

Everyone promptly agreed. Apparently, they'd all seen the thin, sharp-featured man dressed in black, sitting in the back.

"What about him? Does anyone know who he is?" Selma asked.

"He's the family solicitor—the Simple's lawyer. At least that's what Sam Pinager told me before the funeral started. I think he said his name was Graves."

"He's kind of creepy-looking, don't you think?" Mary Addison, the pastor's wife, asked as she applied a portion of shredded lettuce onto each sandwich. "Maybe he's here to investigate the accident further. That bridge is notorious for ice, you know. I always drive slowly across it. Whether it rains or snows, that bridge always has ice on it."

Maggie started to cut the sandwiches into fourths, placing them on the plates provided. She'd been listening to the gossip but, so far, hadn't heard anything to help with her investigation. She decided they needed a bit of prompting.

"So, Dolores's accident needs to be investigated further, does it? Do they think it might not be an accident?" She put the suggestion out there then waited for a response.

Selma was the first to take the bait. "Well, personally, I don't think it was an accident at all."

"What do you mean? Of course, it was an accident!" Mrs. Waterson, an unusually large lady with an unusual-looking blue hat, challenged Selma's remark.

"You all know how Dolores has been, after her husband died of a heart attack," Selma explained. "She's been— *agitated,* to say the least. You know what I mean, we've all seen her around town, acting strangely."

Mary Addison nodded. "I'd call it nervousness…"

"Full of grief…" Mrs. Carter added.

"Anxious…" Sally Henderson said.

There were a few more comments from the women as they vocalized their opinions on the matter. Most just shook their heads in agreement to the remarks. They all seemed to have noticed Dolores's strange behavior around town.

Maggie remained silent but could've added her own word to the list. *Fearful.* That's how Dolores had seemed the day she'd gone to visit her. Dolores had been afraid of something.

"And then there was her worrying about her husband," Selma said.

"You mean, because he'd died earlier?" Mindy Calloway, one of the younger women in the group asked innocently.

"Well, yes—there's that. But she could've been worried about the affair he'd been having."

A gasp of unbelief went through the room.

"I hadn't heard about that." Sandy, the new organist spoke for the first time.

Selma paused. All eyes were upon her now, as if waiting for more information. "I'd heard about an affair," she said, "but really didn't believe it until I saw Mayor Simple in the park with another woman one day."

"Another woman? *Who*?" At least half a dozen voices asked at the same time.

"I was too far away to see who it was, but she had on the tackiest lime-green coat that I've ever seen in my life! You'd think the mayor would have more taste than to be with a woman like that!"

"I've seen him numerous times with the new librarian," Mary Addison chimed in. "Perhaps it was her."

"Me too," Sandy said. "Mayor Simple was always going to the library. He even ate his lunch there, in the park, every day at noon—at least, that's what I've heard."

"Maybe he was just checking out some books—did you ever think of that?" Mrs. Waterson remarked.

"Well, it must've been very upsetting to Dolores, one way or another. If he'd been a loving, loyal husband, Dolores might still be alive today!" Selma exclaimed.

A hush went through the group, then Mindy Calloway quietly said, "So, you're saying that Dolores couldn't live with that anymore, so she decided to... to..." She couldn't bring herself to finish the sentence.

"She decided to what?" Sandy asked innocently, apparently not sure what they were getting at, but before anyone could answer, Mrs. McGinty, the matron of the group, silenced them all.

"Ladies!" she said with a voice full of authority and admonition. "It is inappropriate to talk of such things at a funeral! The verdict was accident, not suicide. And, whether or not the mayor had been meeting with other women—well, that is none of our business whatsoever! We are here today to serve the deceased and her family, not to *gossip* about them. Now, let's get these sandwiches on the tables before the mourners arrive!"

No one dared say another word, not after Mrs. McGinty had spoken. Maggie picked up a tray, feeling justifiably chastised for her own participation in the gossip, and followed the other ladies into the large hall. She moved through the group of people who were just arriving, offering sandwiches to them.

"Are you working here, dear? I thought the local church ladies were providing the luncheon. Has it been catered instead?"

Maggie recognized the booming voice immediately. "Why, Mrs. Barker," she said, turning to see the familiar face. "It's nice to see you here. No, I'm not working—just helping out a bit. I used to live here in Trenton, you know."

"That's right, you did!" Mrs. Barker helped herself to two of the sandwiches. "So, you knew Dolores Simple?"

"Yes, I did. And it seems you did also?"

"She was the star in one of my plays, years ago. It was *The Taming of the Shrew*".

"Really? I had no idea she was in community theatre."

"Yes, she played Katherina to Rob Stanger's Petruchio. Did a very good job of it too. And speaking of the devil…"

Maggie turned to see Rob Stanger this time, dressed uncharacteristically in a suit and tie. "Did I hear someone speak my name?" he casually asked.

"Hi, Rob," Mrs. Barker said as she helped herself to another sandwich. "Nice of you to come. I'm sure Dolores would have appreciated it." She continued to talk as she ate.

Maggie, consumed with thoughts of her own, wasn't paying close attention to her chattering. She was thinking how nice Rob looked in his suit. Suddenly, she realized Mrs. Barker was looking directly at her, waiting for a response. Flustered, Maggie didn't know how to respond. She tried to recall what Mrs. Barker had last said but was at a total loss. Thankfully, Rob came to her rescue. "Yes, Trudy," he said, "do continue telling us all about it." He looked at Maggie and gave her a quick wink.

Mrs. Barker dived in without further prompting. "It was too bad—about Dolores's accident, you know. You never really know what's in store for you, do you? I mean, every morning, we wake and go about our daily lives, working, playing, laughing, being part of humanity—until one day it's all over, just like that!" She tried clicking her fingers for effect, but the sandwich spread had left them a bit slippery. "Then people come to your funeral and say nice things about you that they should've said to you when you were still alive to hear them! Words of praise, of elation, of substance—sharing the essence of our character—words that should've been said before we passed on! Why, it's the wrong-way 'round, isn't it? A mystery of the ages!" She paused for dramatic effect, then slowly added, "Such is life, such is death, and we mortals have no say in the matter, no say whatsoever."

Mrs. Barker solemnly lowered her head. It was an impressive ending to a well-performed soliloquy. A bow would have been appropriate, but she reached for another sandwich instead then moved on towards the dessert table.

"One thing you can say about Trudy Barker," Rob remarked, furtively, "she knows how to make an impressive exit. Are you here to help with the food?"

"I seem to be asked that a lot! No, I'm here as a friend to Dolores—same as you."

"Wish I knew you were going to be here. We could've come together—saved gas and all. You know how they're always wanting us to carpool. Well, I would've done my part to save the planet, if I'd only known."

"Yes, I suppose that would've worked, except I need to be leaving soon to get back home for piano lessons. Perhaps we can carpool the next time there's a funeral?" She smiled jokingly then impulsively handed him the tray of sandwiches. "You wouldn't mind, would you—passing these around for me?"

"Wait… I don't think I can…"

Maggie continued to smile as the mourners began to surround him, trying to choose a sandwich from the tray he was awkwardly holding. Before he could say anything more, she quickly hurried away.

Rob watched her go. He knew he should be irritated but, for some reason or another, was finding himself impressed with her instead.

After a bit more mingling around the room, hoping to find clues for her investigation, Maggie decided it was time to go. She really wasn't cut out for this—didn't know the first thing about what to ask and what to listen for in an investigation—so she collected her coat from the kitchen then stopped by the ladies' room on her way out.

After checking herself in the full-length mirror and reapplying her lipstick, she pushed open the door to leave. She could see two people standing in the hall, just a few yards from the door. One of them was Brad Bennington. He was having a heated argument with a woman in a short black dress and wide-brimmed hat. Maggie quickly backed up inside the ladies' room before they could see her but left the door open a bit to hear what they were saying.

"And if you don't turn over my desk by tomorrow afternoon, you can bet I'll have my lawyers on it!" The woman stamped her foot to show she meant business, but it really had no effect since her foot was clad in the highest heeled shoe Maggie had ever seen.

"I'll concede to the desk, even though Dolores *did* leave everything to me," Brad was calmly telling her. "That's the way it works when one spouse dies before the other. You might've had some claim to it if your brother hadn't been the first to go, but as it is…"

"Dolores didn't own those papers! They belonged to my brother!"

"Yes, and when he died, they were inherited by my sister. And now that she's gone, they're mine. I inherit them!"

"You can't do this to me! I warn you—I'll have my lawyers on this, and you'll be paying through the nose if you don't hand them over now, like a decent human being—if you have any decency in you, that is!"

Maggie listened to the sound of angry footsteps clicking their way down the hall. Then suddenly, the door to the ladies' room was pushed open so forcefully that she had to jump back to avoid being hit. She was astonished at the venomous look on the woman's face as she stormedpast her and disappeared into one of the stalls.

Maggie promptly slipped out of the ladies' room then hurried down the hall towards the exit, only to find herself directly in the path of Brad Bennington! Quickly, she lowered her head and tried to pass him, hoping he wouldn't recognize her.

"Wait! You're the cleaning lady, right?"

Maggie froze, wondering how she was going to explain herself. "I... I was just..."

"And now you're here, helping in the kitchen. I saw you when I arrived, and wanted to thank you for your service."

Maggie let out a sigh of relief. "Glad I could help," was all she could manage to say.

Mr. Bennington seemed genuinely grateful. "Dolores, it seems, had many friends. I'm glad to see that you are one of them." He gave her one last look then left, leaving her standing alone in the hall, her mouth half open.

Maggie quickly recovered her composure then hurried towards the exit, wanting more than ever now to get out of there. Suddenly, she heard someone shouting her name. *What now?* she thought, exasperated.

"Maggie! You're not leaving already, are you?"

Relieved, she saw it was Selma. She was walking towards her, carrying a pitcher of water.

"We sure could use your help if you thought you could stay a bit longer," she said. "Besides, we still have a lot to catch up on. We might not get another chance, you know."

"I'm sorry, but I need to get back to teach piano lessons," Maggie hastily said. "Besides, my mom has had the kids all morning and I really should get back to relieve her if you know what I mean."

"Well, I understand completely. My sister has my kids today and I'll have to admit—I'm glad to be rid of them for a few hours if truth be told! Bet they're giving her fits by now! You know, Maggie, it's been great seeing you again. And, if you ever decide to move back to Trenton, well, here's my card!"

She handed Maggie a business card with *Selma's Real Estate—From House to Home, We'll Secure the Loan!* written on it.

Maggie took it, thinking how inappropriate it was to drum up business at a funeral. She'd forgotten how vigorous Selma was at her profession. She was probably responsible for half the homes sold in Trenton.

"It's been nice seeing you and the other ladies," Maggie told her as she hurried out the door.

"Oh, by the way," she paused briefly, hoping for one last bit of information. "Who's the new librarian you were talking about, earlier? The one who, supposedly, was having an affair with the mayor?"

"Oh, *her.* I don't think you know her—she moved to Trenton about the same time you left. Her name's Candy Turnbull."

CHAPTER EIGHT

Trenton's library was an old, orange brick structure that had been built in the early forties. It was on one level and sat in the middle of the city park. Inside, it had a dozen crowded bookshelves that covered three of the walls, leaving a wide-open area in the middle for the librarian's desk. Candy Turnbull had put a lot of effort into updating the children's section and had installed new tables and chairs there as well as large posters of children's literary characters and seasonal decorations on its walls.

Maggie entered the familiar double doors and was immediately greeted by a blonde woman with short, ratted hair tied with a flamboyant pink scarf.

"May I help you?" she asked.

"Are you the new librarian?" Maggie asked, thinking that this woman was very young—not at all the type Maggie imagined the mayor to be involved with.

"Yes, I'm Candy Turnbull. I was appointed to the position eight months ago when Sylvia Westergard retired."

"I like what you've done with the children's section. The Halloween decorations are great."

"Thank you. The Friends of the Library Committee gave us the funds for it. Fran Knightly, from the city council, was a great help in creating funds for the children's addition too."

"Oh yes, I know Mrs. Knightly well. I used to live here in Trenton but moved to Springville a year ago. I knew Mayor Simple and his wife too. I was sorry to hear of their passing." Maggie watched closely to see Candy Turnbull's reaction to her words.

"Yes, it was very sad," was all she said in reply. Her face was stiff as if she was trying not to show any emotion.

"I worked with Dolores Simple on the Friends of the Library Committee," Maggie told her, "when I lived here, of course."

"Yes, but sadly, the library committee has since been dissolved." Miss Turnbull's voice was suddenly full of disgust. "It's like the town doesn't care anymore about the library! And who could blame them? It's so small and crowded and in desperate need of a renovation. I, personally, would like to see the addition of a computer room. Mayor Simple understood the need to put money into the library. Mrs. Knightly does too, but she's the only one who seems to care. If only Mayor Simple hadn't died."

"Yes. Greg Simple was a good mayor," Maggie agreed with her. "His untimely death affects all who knew him. It sounds like you knew him rather well! Is that right? How well, exactly, did you know him?" Maggie realized, with regret, how eager her words had sounded. She had meant to be more subtle.

Candy Turnbull looked at her accusingly. "You've been listening to the town gossip, haven't you? Well, it's not what you think! Mayor Simple was merely helping me with plans to expand the library—there was nothing personal in it at all! But the planning and fundraising—all the hours of hard work— they came to an end when he died."

Maggie looked at Miss Turnbull sympathetically. "I truly am sorry."

"He died here, in the library park, you know. They say it was his heart. He always sat on the bench under the large oak tree at noon. It's a nice, secluded place, where he could get away from all the city problems for a while and have some time for himself." Candy's voice had become reflective and Maggie listened intently as she spoke. "It does make me wonder, though."

"Why? What do you wonder? Could his death have been caused by something other than a heart attack?"

Candy Turnbull stared at Maggie, her eyes cold and hostile again. "Why, exactly, did you come to the library today? Certainly not to talk about the past mayor!"

Maggie quickly pulled a book out of her purse. She had gotten it from Janie's room that morning and had brought it as a prop—just in case she needed a reason for being there.

"I think this might belong to the library. I found it, after we moved, among my daughter's things." She handed it over to Miss Turnbull.

Candy looked it over carefully then gave it back to Maggie. "Thanks for being—well, conscientious—but this isn't one of ours."

"Are you sure? Do you want to check your listings?"

"No, I know all the books here. We don't have that many, as you can see for yourself."

Maggie handed the book back to Miss Turnbull. "Then, I'd like to donate it to your library, if that's all right."

Miss Turnbull seemed genuinely grateful. Hesitantly, she thanked Maggie for the book.

"Nice little library you have here!" A familiar voice came booming through the double doors, interrupting their conversation. It was Rob Stanger, walking in with his usual air of confidence.

"What are you doing here!?" Maggie exclaimed, with some annoyance in her voice. "We seem to keep running into each other."

"Why, it's Maggie Brown! I could ask you the same question, you know. You haven't been following me, have you?"

"Now, that's not fair, seeing how I was here first! Perhaps it's you who's following me!"

He ignored the comment. "Seriously, though—I didn't expect to see you here in Trenton."

"I don't know why. I often visit the library."

"We have a perfectly good library in Springville, you know. Why come all the way to Trenton to check out a book when we've got one in our own town?"

Miss Turnbull discreetly bowed out of the conversation, leaving the two of them alone to talk.

Maggie watched her silent retreat before attempting to answer Rob's question.

"I used to live here," she told him, "and after returning a long overdue book, I stayed awhile to talk to the new librarian. Now, what are *you* doing here? You don't live here either."

"Can we discuss this outside?" Rob said, taking her by the arm and leading her out of the door.

"Wait a minute! Stop pulling me!" Maggie demanded. "Just what do you think you're doing?"

"Trying not to let you blow my cover, that's what," he said when they got outside. "I'm working undercover, you might say—doing a bit of investigating."

Maggie was surprised. "What do you mean, you're *investigating?* Just what, or who are you investigating? It's not the new librarian, is it?"

"It might be."

"Who hired you?"

"Sorry, but that's confidential."

"Or, in other words, none of my business."

"Since you put it that way, yes." Rob quickly led her over to a bench, secluded by a large oak tree. "Look, I'm sorry for dragging you out here. I might have overreacted."

"Do you think?"

"Well, really, why *are* you here? Seriously, Maggie, it does look a bit—odd, that you came all the way to Trenton for the silly reasons you gave me."

Maggie tried to act offended, but knew Rob was seeing right through it. She wondered if she should tell him the real reason for her visit to Trenton's library today.

"Would you believe that I needed to check out a book?"

Rob looked at her, suspiciously. "What book?"

"*War and Peace?*"

"*War and Peace*? Really?"

"Okay, so it wasn't *War and Peace*. But, actually— have you ever read that book before?"

"Perhaps for a school assignment?" Maggie tested one of her mother's tactics by trying to change the subject.

"No, I haven't. You know, now that I think of it, it was on the list of books to choose from in high school, but I chose something shorter—I think it was *The Red Badge of Courage.*" He suddenly stopped, seeing the smile spread on Maggie's face and knowing he'd fallen for her trap. "Now stop trying to change the subject!" he said, irritated. "So, you don't want to tell me why you came here. Okay, that's fair enough— especially since I'm not telling you everything either— so we should just leave it at that."

"You came to check out the librarian," Maggie reminded him.

"Wow, I haven't heard that line since *The Music Man* premiered in our local theatre."

"Well, believe it or not, that's why I came too. You see, I have reason to believe that Mayor Simple's death might have been—well, *murder.*" Maggie had a little trouble saying the word out loud, not sure she really believed it herself. "And, since he was involved with this new librarian, I came to find out what I could."

Maggie was surprised at Rob's reaction. He put his head back and started to laugh.

"Now, wait a minute," she protested. "I don't think this is funny at all!"

"No," Rob said, "it isn't—not really. But it looks like we're both on the same mission—investigating Mayor Simple through his connection to the librarian. How about we pool our resources—you know—work together on this."

Maggie was surprised. "I... I don't know..."

"Well, we should! And why not? We could cover a lot more ground that way."

"I'm not a private detective, you know."

"No, but what has that got to do with anything?"

Maggie paused to consider Rob's proposal, still smarting a bit from his laughter. "Tell you what, Rob," she said, "you go back into that library and find out what you can, and I'll get into my car and drive back to Springville and think it over. I'll let you know my decision tonight at play practice."

"That works for me," Rob said, agreeably. "See you tonight."

Maggie remained seated on the bench, watching him leave. *The nerve,* she thought to herself.

Grilling me as if I were a suspect, then laughing at my answer! Angrily she stood, ready to leave herself. As she did, her foot caught on something lying on the ground—something that stuck into the sole of her soft canvas shoe. She bent down to retrieve it and saw it was a tie pin. It had a figure of a dolphin on the front, all stretched out in a graceful dive.

Maggie detached it from her shoe then picked it up. *Now, where have I seen this before?* The pin looked strangely familiar, but she couldn't recall why. She really didn't want to go back inside the library to place it in the lost and found, so she dropped it in her purse instead. Maybe next trip she would, but not today—not with Rob still there.

"Before I draw nearer to that stone to which you point, answer me one question. Are these the shadows of things that Will be, or are they shadows of things that May be, only?"

The ghost of Christmas future pointed downward to the grave by which it stood, solemn and immovable.

"Men's courses will foreshadow certain ends, to which, if persevered in, they must lead. But if the courses be departed from, the ends will change."

Scrooge stood on the darkened stage and watched as the tall, ominous figure remained in the shadows on stage right. Then, slowly, he crept towards the gravestone. The spotlight followed him until it rested upon the stone, showing the name to be his own. The words *Ebenezer Scrooge* were engraved upon it in bold, threatening letters.

"Am I that man who lay upon the bed?" he asked, falling upon his knees repentantly and imploring the ominous spirit to answer. But the figure remained mute, pointing only a bony finger at the grave.

"No, Spirit. Oh no, no..." The music suddenly became louder, its minor tones cadencing to a climax.

"And...cut!" Mrs. Barker's voice bellowed from the side of the stage. "Wait! We need darkness here! The lights have got to be cut too! Carson? Michael? Are you up there or have you fallen sleep again?!"

"We're here!" Two teenage voices crackled simultaneously from somewhere above. Suddenly, the lights went out, leaving the stage in total darkness.

"Okay, that's good." Mrs. Barker was satisfied with the black out. "Carson, bring the lights up now and everyone, on stage for the finale!"

An hour later, after the last scene of the show had been practiced at least a dozen times or more, Rob Stanger made his way over to the piano. He was anxious to hear what Maggie had decided. He felt a bit guilty though, knowing he really couldn't include her in his investigation. He'd only asked her to so he could discover what she knew about Trenton's librarian. Pushing the thought aside, he also knew that pretending to work with Maggie was a good way to get to know her better. There was something about her that he couldn't quite put his finger on, and what better way to discover it than to have an excuse to be around her as often as possible.

He was disappointed to see Mrs. Barker had gotten there first. She was sitting on the bench next to Maggie, working out cuts in the music.

"We really need to tighten things up a bit, you know—this play is much too long for our audience. We need them to leave wanting more instead of bored because it was too long!"

Mrs. Barker had a red pencil in her hand and was ruthlessly slashing the measures of music she determined unnecessary. "Measures twenty-two through thirty-six can easily be cut here in the incidental music, and on page nineteen just after the dance, we can take out these four lines that lead to the coda."

Maggie watched silently as Mrs. Barker crossed out the offending measures, wishing she'd known sooner of their demise before spending time practicing them. As soon as Mrs. Barker was content with the reduction, she swung herself off the bench so suddenly that she ran smack dab into Rob Stanger who'd been lingering behind her.

"Oh Rob—didn't see you! Why are you always standing by the piano?!" Mrs. Barker glanced over at Maggie, realizing at once why he was standing there. She hurried away, trying not to get in the middle of another theatrical romance. After all, they seemed to happen regularly, every time she put on a play. If she paid much attention to them, it would distract her from the matter at hand—to put on the best play possible. Still, it was quite the sacrifice for someone who loved a good gossip, as she did.

Maggie collected her music, knowing she was late in getting home. Tonight's rehearsal had been unusually long and tedious. Rob followed her across the theatre and out the door.

"Can I walk you home?" he asked. "Remember, we were going to talk about working together."

"That wouldn't be too practical, you know," Maggie told him.

"And why not? You seemed more agreeable at the library park! What's changed your mind?"

Maggie looked at him, confused. "I think we're talking about two different things," she said. "I'd love to work with you on the investigation. But I don't think it's a good idea for you to walk me home."

"And why is that?"

"Because you'd have to come back for your jeep, that's why." She pointed to the red 1980 Wrangler parked across the street.

Rob looked a bit sheepish. "Then, how about you let me drive you home? We really need some time to talk things over. I can get the jeep warmed up and bring it over. You just wait here."

"No, really, I want to walk. I need some fresh air to clear my head, especially after the rehearsal tonight."

"I know what you mean. It does get a bit intense after all the blocking is done. How about I walk you part of the way so we can talk?"

Maggie relented and soon they were walking side by side, discussing Rob's case. "Did you find out anything—you know, about the librarian?" she asked.

"Candy Turnbull is a very disappointed young lady," Rob stated. "Apparently, the mayor had promised to put a good deal of money towards the library—money that's not going to come through now that he's dead. When the mayor died, so did Miss Turnbull's hope of a renovation."

"I see." Maggie was suddenly interested. "Did she say where the money was coming from?"

"No, she was pretty close-mouthed about that. I'm guessing, though, that the city had come into some unexpected money and that the mayor was trying to get the council to approve giving it to the library. How about you? Did you find out anything worthwhile? Perhaps we can meet, sometime after working hours, to discuss it."

"Working hours? Just where do you work? I thought you were a private investigator. Do they have working hours?"

"I also teach criminal law at the university. The detective work is just a part time thing."

Maggie was impressed but wasn't about to show him. "Waiting to decide what you want to be when you grow up?" she taunted.

"Yeah, something like that."

"I don't mean to change the subject, but I wish you'd tell me who hired you to investigate this. It wasn't my mother, was it?" Maggie was starting to wonder just how far her mother would go in getting her to date again.

Rob laughed. "Your mother? What a funny thing to say." He looked at Maggie curiously and the spoke. "But tell me, why are *you* looking into this? Maybe I'm missing something, but I don't see how the mayor's death has anything to do with you."

"It really doesn't, except that Dolores Simple—more or less —asked me to. Maggie went on to explain how fearful Dolores had been at their last meeting and the strange request she'd made about papers in her broom closet.

"She told you about some *papers?* And you dressed up as a maid to retrieve them?" Rob began laughing out loud.

"I don't see why that's so funny!" Maggie protested, wondering why he laughed at her so much. Was she really that pathetic? She stopped suddenly. "This is half-way."

Rob stared at her. There was more to Maggie Brown than met the eyes. "When can I come over and have a look at those papers?"

"You can come Saturday night, if you want."

"Saturday? Hmmm. Isn't that Halloween?"

"Yes, it is. And if you come, I'll save you a caramel apple. Do you like caramel?"

"Of course—who doesn't? Even more so when it's stuck on a nice, crisp apple."

"Then I'll meet you on my back porch. Does nine-thirty work for you? That gives me enough time to get the kids in bed after trick-or-treating. I live in the house, just there, past the streetlight."

Rob was intrigued. "Sounds a bit clandestine to me. On your porch at nine-thirty. Do I need to wear a rosebud in my lapel? How about a password? Will I need one to get past your overly suspecting mother?"

Maggie gave him a look of reproof. "If you don't want to come…"

"I'll be there!"

Without another word, he turned and crunched his way back down the sidewalk through the leaves. Maggie walked the rest of the way home alone, trying to decide where all this was going.

She decided it didn't really matter. Her mother had been right. Even if there was nothing to the papers she had found, even if Dolores's accident proved to be just that—an accident, she was starting to have some fun along the way. She smiled, feeling a bit guilty.

CHAPTER NINE

Halloween had arrived, the season of mischief. At dusk, groups of children began to form on neighboring doorsteps, dressed in costumes and ready to gather in a harvest of their own sugary treats.

Janie and Susan were dressed, respectively, as Mary Poppins and Cinderella. Maggie had put an old sheet over Wesley's warm coat, then made dark circles around his eyes with her eye shadow. A ghost riding in a stroller, holding his plastic pumpkin, would do for him. Grandma stayed behind to pass out caramel apples to the neighborhood kids.

Excitement was in the air as they made their way to the nearby houses. The air also had a definite tinge of coldness to it, and although the children seemed able to ignore it, it was reminding the grownups of the coming winter. Maggie came prepared herself, wearing a jacket over her sweater and had her children all bundled up under their costumes as well.

Sofie's was the first house to visit, just across the street. When they rang her doorbell, she sprung open her door so fast that it made Maggie jump. Candy Corn immediately sneaked out and padded her way over to Susan who was walking up the porch, ready to receive a treat. Candy Corn mewed, demanding her attention.

"Trick-or-Treat!" Susan and Janie shouted in unison.

"It's Louisa's grandkids from across the street—little Janie and Susan! Don't you look sweet?" Sofie gushed. "And there's our little Wesley, all dressed up like a ghost!"

Sofie's round frame was clothed in a brightly-colored skirt that went all the way to the floor. She had on long, dangling earrings that flashed in the porchlight, and even longer necklaces that glittered across her ruffled blouse. Maggie wondered what her costume was supposed to be. A gypsy, perhaps?

"Tell Miss Sofie, thank you," Maggie prompted her kids after they each received a tootsie roll from the large orange bowl Sofie was holding. Susan bent down to pick up Candy Corn then handed her over to her owner. Sofie fumbled as she tried to hold Candy Corn in one arm and the treat bowl in the other.

"Be careful, kids!" she hollered after them, then retreated into her house to lie in wait for the next group of revelers.

Maggie and her small entourage spent the next hour or so working the right side of the neighborhood before venturing off into places not so well-known, collecting candy at each house along the way. It wasn't long before their bags were starting to get a bit heavy. "After this house," she told them, "we should start back home. We can do all the houses on the other side of the road on our way back."

"Mommy, did you see what that lady gave us?" Janie was impressed by her first full-size candy bar.

"Yes, I did. Watch your step there, Janie!"

Two older boys, dressed as Indiana Jones, were coming down a porch. They almost knocked Janie over in their haste to get to the next house. Maggie hurried over to help.

"Hello, Maggie! Out with the kids tonight, are you?" Maggie looked up to see an old hag with a long, crooked nose talking to her at the bottom of the step. The hag wore a long black dress with a purple cape and a pointed witches' hat.

"Mrs. Barker? Is that you?" Maggie realized that this old hag had no resemblance whatsoever to Trudy Barker but the booming voice coming from her was unmistakable.

"I'm taking my nephews trick-or-treating tonight, so I thought I'd wear a costume. It's from one of my plays."

"Let me guess. Shakespeare's *Macbeth*?"

"Spot on!"

Maggie walked to the next house with Mrs. Barker and her nephews. While the children went up the porch to ring the doorbell, Trudy Barker began doing the one thing that she did so well, apart from directing plays. She began to gossip.

"...and the teller at the bank—do you know her? She lives a block over from main, the house with the blue shutters and the yellow rosebush on the side. Well, she told her boyfriend to buy her a ring or else. They were at the playhouse last night and Vanna was displaying the largest diamond I've ever seen! I suspect, though, that it's really zirconium."

Maggie smiled. Mrs. Barker was in her element.

"She's Benson's granddaughter—you know—Benson from the play? When his wife died, ages ago—I think she had a stroke or something—well, he moved into Springville from Trenton at that time, to live with his son and daughter-in-law— not Vanna, but the other one. He started to build sets for the playhouse then and has been doing it ever since."

Maggie was suddenly interested. "Benson used to live in Trenton? I had no idea."

"Oh, yes. He raised quite the family there—seven children in all. Was active in community affairs too. Of course, he's retired now—to our advantage—he has a lot of time to help us with the sets. Did you know he paints the background scenes for our plays as well? And his son comes too, to help every now and then. At least, when his wife lets him."

Maggie was making a mental note to talk to Benson about Trenton's earlier days. Perhaps he'd know something about the hospital committee.

"I wanted to tell you how much you're appreciated at the playhouse," Mrs. Barker continued. "Everyone tells me how much they like you there. They say, 'Maggie Brown is so much better than'—well—than the last accompanist was. Did you know her, Phyllis Tinney? She moved to West Belview to help with her aging mother. It was the best move she ever made, at least for us at the playhouse!"

Maggie was a bit embarrassed by the praise. "I'm glad to be there," was all she could think to say.

"I should warn you, though," her voice suddenly became hushed as if she was telling Maggie a secret of vital importance. "Rob Stanger likes you. Did you know?"

"I thought you said everybody at the playhouse likes me," Maggie replied, trying to brush off the remark. She'd wondered about that herself. Rob seemed to be spending a lot of time with her.

"Yes, everybody likes you, dear. But he really is falling for you, and fast."

Maggie was speechless. How was she expected to respond to that?

"Here's where we part, Maggie, dear. We've already done those houses. It's been nice talking to you. Boys! This way!" Mrs. Barker crossed the street suddenly, with her nephews hurrying after her. "See you next week at rehearsal!"

Maggie waved goodbye, secretly glad to be going in the opposite direction of Trudy Barker and her candid remarks.

Maggie got her kids all settled down for the night a bit later than usual, then waited alone on the back porch for Rob to come. She was holding the folder that contained the hospital minutes, determined to keep this meeting with him as short and business-like as possible. She decided that she'd just hand him the folder, let him look through the papers inside, and then be done with it. If Mrs. Barker was right, and he was falling for her, she'd put an end to it fast by not encouraging him or giving him any reason to stay later than necessary.

Good as his word, Rob arrived at exactly nine-thirty.

"Are those the papers you took from Dolores Simples' house?" he asked, sounding a bit too eager. He was relieved when Maggie didn't seem to notice.

"I know I shouldn't have taken them." Maggie was at once on the defense. "It's just that, Dolores did tell me to, in a way."

"Hey, you don't have to explain anything to me. I'm actually impressed that you went to her house and found them." He sat down on the step next to her. "May I have a look at them?"

Maggie handed him the folder and waited while he looked over each paper, on at a time, by the light coming through the kitchen window.

"Why these are just some minutes from a hospital meeting!" he exclaimed, disappointed. "And, look at that date—why, they're forty years old!" He hurriedly put the papers back inside the folder and handed them to Maggie. "Why in the world would you think these were important?"

Maggie was starting to get defensive but tried to explain. "I thought they were important because Dolores said they were. There was no other reason." She waited for Rob to say something.

"Are you sure these are the papers that Dolores told you about, because if they are, she must've been out of her mind! These aren't at all what I expected!"

"Just what were you expecting?" Maggie asked, suspiciously.

Rob looked at her and was immediately sorry for reacting the way he had. "The only thing I was expecting tonight," he said, his voice calmer now, "was one of your caramel apples. You did say you'd save me one."

"Yes, I did," Maggie said without emotion. "I'll see if there are any left."

Rob followed her through the door and into the kitchen, thinking hard how he could remedy the situation. He knew he'd been much too eager about seeing the papers and, although he was disappointed to find they weren't what he'd hoped for, knew he couldn't change that now.

Still, he might be able to get back on Maggie's good side yet.

"You know, Maggie," he began slowly, "if we could find someone who'd been on the hospital committee back then, well, perhaps we could find out if these have any value."

Maggie had found the leftover caramel apples on a tray by the sink. She placed one of them on the table in front of Rob, still angry with him.

"Do you know anyone from Trenton who might know the people on that committee?" Rob glanced at her and thought he saw her soften a bit.

"Well, Mrs. Barker told me that Benson was from Trenton. He might know. And, then there's Mrs. Knightly. She's on the city council in Trenton. She's pretty old—has been in city government forever. Perhaps she could tell us something."

"Yes, that's an idea!" Rob was relieved at her response. She was finally coming around. "We could go there together, for a visit. Of course, we can't tell her the real reason we're asking, not without getting into the business of you taking the minutes from Dolores's house, but I bet you can think of something to tell her. If that doesn't pan out, we can always talk to Benson at play practice."

Maggie thought about his plan. "Mrs. Knightly doesn't know *you*, so if she does ask—well, you could tell her you're doing some investigative journalism. Isn't that sort of what you teach at the college?"

"Keeping some truth in it, yes, I see what you're getting at." Once again, he was impressed at Maggie's ingenuity. "I say we do it! How about I pick you up on Monday morning and we drive to Trenton to see what the old gal knows?"

Rob noticed that Maggie was smiling again. *At least that was something,* he thought. And, at least he could spend more time with her on Monday when they made the trip to Trenton.

CHAPTER TEN

A large, mahogany desk was delivered to Coralee Simple's elegant apartment in downtown Chesterville. The antique looked out of place in the modern décor of vertical blinds and shag carpeting that dominated the room. Nevertheless, Coralee was excited to see the old family heirloom. She also felt relieved it had come. After the funeral, she'd had her doubts that Dolores's brother would honor her wish and let her have the desk. But in the long run, he'd caved into her threats and now the desk was hers, as well it should be!

She opened each drawer, one at a time, only to shut them again when she found they were empty. Dolores's brother had been very thorough in emptying it out—probably searching for the missing papers himself. At least he *thought* he'd been thorough. Coralee smiled to herself. Mr. Bradley Bennington hadn't known about one little thing. It was something she'd known about ever since she was a little child watching her grandfather at work. There was a hidden drawer in this old desk, and she knew how to open it!

Her long, slender fingers felt inside the small drawer at the top, searching for a lever. There it was, at the very back. When she pushed it, a smaller drawer—one that didn't even look like a drawer because it was so well hidden in the elaborate carvings—popped open. Once again, her finger pushed its hidden lever and magically, another drawer—a long vertical one, that lay just below the surface of the desk, opened an inch or so. Coralee smiled as she pulled the drawer out the rest of the way then smiled even bigger when she saw what she'd been looking for inside its hidden compartment.

She silently thanked her dead brother for his conscientious effort in hiding these precious papers so well. Now that she'd found them, there was just one more thing to do. She quickly dialed a number and waited for an answer.

"Hello, this is Coralee Simple. I'm at 241 Ivy Lane Drive, number 17. Yes, that's right, I'm the one with a 1920 Chippendale writing desk. Could you send someone along to pick it up? Yes, I'd like an appraisal. What's that? Wednesday at 2:00? Yes, I'll be waiting for you then."

She hung up the phone and walked back into the living room. Now that the desk had given up its secret, it had to go. Something so out-of-date just wouldn't fit in with her modern apartment—this beautiful penthouse that she had so painstakingly decorated herself. But, giving it away was out of the question too. After all, it was an heirloom, owned at one time by her beloved grandfather and should be worth a lot of money. She'd see what she could get for it from the auction house first. The old desk might fetch at least a thousand or two —nothing to compare with what she'd found inside its hidden drawer, but still, a thousand dollars was nothing to sneeze at. After collecting what the papers would fetch, the money she could expect from the sale of the desk would be the proverbial icing on the cake.

A knock came at the door. Coralee peered through the peephole to see who it was then opened it, trying to control her anger.

"So, it's *you*," she said. "First, at the funeral, then here. What is it, exactly, that you want from me?"

Malcolm Graves walked in. "I see you got the desk," he stated, walking closer towards it to get a better look at the impressive antique Coralee had.

Coralee hurried past him, then casually placed a book over the papers she'd left upon it, hoping to conceal them from his view. Malcolm noticed her feeble attempt at subterfuge and couldn't help but comment. "What's this you're trying to hide? You don't need to have any secrets from me."

Coralee feigned a laugh. "Just a letter from a secret admirer —really none of your business."

Malcolm Graves moved away from the desk towards Coralee's lush sofa. Without waiting for an invitation, he sat himself down and casually crossed his long, thin legs. Irritated, Coralee asked him, once again, why he was there.

"It's a little matter of a signature," he said as he pulled a folded paper from his black suit pocket and placed it on the coffee table in front of her. He then produced a gold-embossed pen from his jacket. Clicking it on, he handed it to her.

Coralee glanced at the paper. "Oh, *this*," she said. "I hope this will be the last of the little misunderstanding we got ourselves into."

"A misunderstanding, huh? That's the first time I've heard a marriage called that before. Just what do you think was misunderstood? How about we call it a mistake instead and leave it at that. And yes, this is the last thing you'll have to sign. Our divorce is now final—well, as soon as I get this back to the lawyer."

Eagerly, she took the pen and signed the document. "Now, if there isn't anything else, I've got somewhere I need to be."

Malcolm took his time getting off the sofa then leisurely strolled towards the door, getting a quick glance at the desk again. He suddenly walked over to it and brushed a hand over its surface. "What are your plans for this?" he asked casually.

Coralee opened the front door. "The desk?" she inquired, hoping he didn't mean the papers on top of it.

"Of course, the desk. What else would I be talking about?"

"It's none of your business, dear." She opened the door wider. "Now, please, it's time for you to leave!"

As soon as he was gone and the door carefully bolted once again, Coralee opened the secret drawer and replaced the papers inside the hidden compartment. *That was a close call*, she thought, and it wouldn't do to take any more chances. The papers needed to remain safely hidden until she was ready to sell them, which should be sooner than later, all things considered.

"Please, come in." Mrs. Knightly opened the door, welcoming her two guests. "Maggie Brown," she stated, "how nice to see you. And this must be Rob Stanger."

Fran Knightly was an unusual combination of quaint old lady and shrewd businesswoman. At the age of sixty-three, she'd inherited her husband's furniture company when he'd died suddenly from complications following surgery. That was eighteen years ago, and she was still going strong. She'd taken her husband's place as president of the company as well as his place on the city council, showing more aptitude than he'd ever shown in either of the roles. Yet, she was still all lace, tea and crumpets. It was quite the contrast in one elegant, white-haired old lady.

She told them to sit. There were two Victorian style chairs in the room, a matching loveseat, and a pastel lemon colored sofa. All had matching lace doilies on the arms and backs. A tray of assorted sandwiches and scones sat atop a lavishly carved coffee table in the center of the room.

Next to that an antique porcelain tea-set, complete with teapot and cups, a cream pitcher and sugar bowl, was displayed —each piece decorated with tiny pink, hand painted roses.

"If you both sit on the loveseat you can reach the sandwiches better. That's right. Now, help yourselves—I've made plenty." She began to pour the tea out into each dainty cup then politely inquired whether they wanted sugar and cream. After all the necessary formalities, they settled down to the refreshments and small talk.

"Just what is it that you do, Mr. Stanger?" she graciously asked.

"I teach law at the university."

"And he plays Scrooge in Springville's *A Christmas Carol*", Maggie added, hoping to distract Mrs. Knightly from asking too many questions about Rob's vocation. It wouldn't do to let her know he was a private investigator. "You should come and see the play," Maggie continued. "They've got me in it too— well, accompanying on the piano."

"Yes, I've gone to Springville in years past to see the plays. They're quite good for an amateur playhouse. Perhaps I'll come again."

"You wouldn't be disappointed if you did. But get your ticket early—they sell out quickly!" Rob eagerly added.

Mrs. Knightly nodded. "You know, Maggie, we really miss having you here in our community. A good accompanist is hard to come by. Do you do much accompanying in Springville? Besides the community theatre, that is."

"Not a lot, but I have started to teach piano there. I have fourteen students, mostly from the neighborhood."

"Are you *enjoying* it?" Mrs. Knightly seemed a bit doubtful that anyone could enjoy teaching a musical instrument to a child.

"It's fine," Maggie replied, not sure how she really felt about it, if truth be known. "I enjoy having a job that keeps me close to my own children," she added.

"And you teach at the university? That's a noble profession." Mrs. Knightly had turned her attention back to Rob now, wanting to know more about the good-looking man sitting in front of her.

"Yes, I've been teaching there for about six years. If you've got to work, it's as good a job as any. The pay isn't all that great but then, the big paying jobs tend to keep you so busy you don't have time for anything else."

"Like, playing Scrooge at the local theatre," Mrs. Knightly added.

"Yes, exactly. All work and no play—well, you know how that ends up!"

Mrs. Knightly nodded in agreement. "Now, what is it that's brought you here today?" She seemed ready to be done with the small talk and move onto the real reason behind their visit. "Is there something you want me to do—other than come to your play?"

Maggie looked at Rob. He sat silently, indicating that she should lead the way, so she jumped in.

"We were hoping you could tell us what you know about the hospital board—the one that was created in 1941 to raise money to build Trenton's hospital. We're especially interested in the committee members. I already know about one—her name is Thelma Greeley." Maggie named the one person who was listed on the papers she had. "She was spear-heading a fund drive for it."

Mrs. Knightly smiled. "And you thought of me because I've been around for a long time and might remember? Well, let me see if I can help."

Rob glanced at Maggie. He could see how hopeful she was, but nervous as well.

"When the city decided to build the hospital, a committee was formed to find the necessary funds to make it happen, just like you said. That was, let's see, I believe it was in 1940. Its members put together some plans to present to the city council —plans on how to raise the funds for the hospital to be built. However, a year later, before the building was even started, it was bought by a private company, so the committee was dissolved."

"Do you remember anyone on the committee? Thelma Greeley, perhaps?" Maggie asked.

"It was so long ago—and it really didn't have anything to do with me. At the time I wasn't even involved with the city council, although my husband was. But I can ask around a bit and let you know what I find out. I can tell you one thing for a surety. Your Mrs. Greeley is no longer with us. She passed on, oh… it's been at least twenty years or so. She was very active in community affairs, right up until her death. May I ask why you are interested in something that happened so long ago?"

"I'm the one interested," Rob spoke. "It's for a project I'm doing—for one of my classes."

"Ah, yes, at the university, as you mentioned before." Mrs. Knightly nodded her head, seemingly content with his answer. Without any further question about the committee, she moved on to another topic. "Now, you must tell me, Maggie, how you and your young man here met."

Maggie was surprised. Why would Mrs. Knightly think she was dating Rob? "No, no…it's not like that at all," she tried to explain. "Rob is, well… he's a friend I met at the community theatre."

"Are you sure, dear? What about you, Rob? Why would a young man like you settle for being Maggie's friend when you could date her? I'm afraid the world has passed me by. I just don't understand the 'rules' of courtship anymore!"

Rob remained quiet, secretly enjoying watching Maggie squirm.

"We really should be going now." Maggie stood, all flustered, ready for this turn of the conversation to end. "Thank you so much for your time and the lovely tea. I can't tell you how much… how much…"

She suddenly dropped back down on the loveseat, her legs giving out on her. The town siren had started to sound, signaling its warning to Trenton's paramedics and firemen and summoning them to a new emergency. It came screaming back into Maggie's memory, reminding her of the night Wesley was born, the night she'd lost Hal. She started shaking uncontrollably.

Concerned, Rob held her while Mrs. Knightly ran to get a cold washcloth. When she returned, she placed the washcloth on Maggie's forehead then proceeded to tell Rob how to prop her feet up on a nearby stool.

"Lay still, dear, and keep your feet elevated."

The siren kept up its blaring noise for another half a minute or so before it finally subsided, leaving the room unusually silent. Maggie, regaining control of herself, suddenly felt very foolish. She sat up, making the washcloth drop onto her lap and her head spin.

"I'm so sorry...I feel like such an idiot!" she said, trying to explain. "You see, it happened the night my husband, Hal, died...the siren. It sounded then, just before I went to the hospital. And now, I seem to relive that night every time I hear it."

"Don't think anything of it, dear," Mrs. Knightly said in a soothing voice. "I can't tell you how much I hate that siren myself! In fact, I've been trying for years to get the city council's vote to put an end to it, but nobody is willing to cooperate. It's been a tradition in Trenton for too many years."

"I understand why it's needed though," Maggie bravely said. "How else would the firemen and paramedics know there's an emergency if it wasn't for the siren warning them?"

"Our firemen and paramedics have all had pagers for years now, letting them know when to come to an emergency!" Mrs. Knightly had suddenly become very animated. "It's certain *people* who want to keep the siren—the busybodies in town! Although it's outdated and seriously archaic—it's an air-raid siren from World War II, after all—those highly vocal citizens want to keep it so they'll know when something important is happening, and the city council is too lazy to stand up to them!"

Maggie handed Mrs. Knightly the washcloth that had fallen onto her lap. Rob, concerned, helped her to stand. Although Mrs. Knightly had been very kind about the whole thing, Maggie was still embarrassed and wanted to leave as soon as possible.

Mrs. Knightly promised to call Maggie if she found any information about the hospital committee. Rob helped Maggie down the front steps and into his jeep then drove slowly out of town. He'd brought her here, not caring about the papers she'd found in the least, but with his own agenda to fulfill—to spend some time with her. Now something was bothering him, something he couldn't seem to shake. Was he starting to fall for her?

As soon as they left, Mrs. Knightly picked up the phone and dialed a familiar number.

"Hello, Daisy? Fran Knightly here. Is Dick in? Yes, I need to talk to him. Thank you, I'll wait." Mrs. Knightly proceeded to pace back and forth while she waited, as far as the phone cord would allow. Soon Daisy was back on the other line.

"He's not in? Then have him call me back as soon as possible." Mrs. Knightly didn't even try to hide her agitation. "I've got something important to tell him."

CHAPTER ELEVEN

Trenton city offices were located just off main street, next to the senior center. The one-story brick building was set in pleasant surroundings of trees and lawn, with a flowerbed by the entrance. In the foyer, a large glass case held pictures of all the mayors since 1955. The justice court was straight on past the foyer through orange painted doors. It was held in the same room as the city council met. Other small offices—one for the mayor, the city manager, and the city clerk—were just down the hall. Daisy Armstrong, the receptionist and secretary, sat behind a desk in the front office, directing people to the various departments and taking utility payments over the counter.

Dick Wood, the city manager, and Jay Lindt, the city clerk, had just gotten back from lunch. They checked in with Daisy to see if there had been any calls for them.

"Just Florence Watson, wondering when the new mayor will be appointed," Daisy said, rolling her eyes. "It's the fourth time she's called this week. Oh, and your wife called too, Dick, reminding you to pick up your daughter from dance practice on your way home tonight. Jay, would you cover the front desk for me while I go to lunch? It *is* 2:30.”

Jay looked at his watch, surprised it was so late. “I guess we took a longer lunch than we'd planned. Maybell's was swamped today, and you know how short staffed they get sometimes, especially at lunch.”

“Maybe I should get a job there,” Daisy retorted.

Jay laughed. “Only if you want to work during your lunch hour.”

“Seems like I do that already!” Daisy grabbed her coat and purse then quickly headed for the door before anything else could stop her from going. “Looks like someone's coming in to pay her bill,” she announced as she ducked out the door, leaving Jay to handle it.

“Kelli Sanderson!” Dick greeted the familiar face, opening the door to let her in. “I thought you were always at the hospital working a non-stop shift. It's good to see you out doing something else for a change.”

Nurse Kelli smiled. “Yes, they do keep me busy. Is Jay here today?”

“Right there, behind the counter. He's covering for Daisy.”

Dick headed down the hall towards his own office, leaving Jay to handle Nurse Kelli and her bill.

“Hi, Jay. Looks like you're pulling double duty today. Where was Daisy heading just now? She's not taking off early, is she?”

“No, she's just taking a late lunch. Do you want to pay your utility bill? I can take care of it, if you'd like.” Jay's voice was unusually formal, as if he were reciting lines in a play.

“He's inside his office now,” Kelli whispered over the counter. “You can stop the act.”

Jay let out a sigh of relief. Kelli asked, "So, are we still on for Sunday?"

"I'm planning on it. What time should I pick you up?"

"It all depends on what you have in mind. Dinner perhaps, before the movie?"

"How about dinner *afterwards,* if the movie isn't too long. That will give us enough time to get you back to the hospital for your shift."

"I really enjoyed last Tuesday. I hadn't been skating for years! And Chinese take-out afterwards, at your place—it was really the perfect date!"

"So, perhaps Sunday is unnecessary, now that we've achieved perfection?"

Kelli laughed. "You can't get out of it that easily. Besides, I've asked for the night off, so we could have that dinner you suggested and whatever else you think we have time for." She blew him a kiss over the counter then waved provocatively. "See you on Sunday!"

Jay watched as she left the building, a bit concerned. He turned on the overhead fan, hoping to blow away the smell of perfume that always remained after she left. He remembered his blue sweater and how the smell had lingered there for months, even after he'd had it cleaned.

"Are we to expect an announcement soon?" Dick suddenly appeared from out of nowhere. He'd heard the end of the conversation and was ready to give Jay a bit of razzing.

Jay tried not to be bothered. "No, definitely not."

"Just having a bit of fun, then? I'm not one to judge, but I wouldn't get too serious if I was planning on dropping her in the end—no, not our Nurse Kelli. I'll bet you anything that she'd have you drawn and quartered if you tried to break up with her, and then she'd do something really mean!"

"Don't worry. I can handle it."

"I hope so. I'd hate to lose our city recorder just before the year-end report is finished."

"Very funny, Dick."

"By the way, Mrs. Knightly called me again."

"Let me guess, she wants the town siren retired. Doesn't she know how much our citizens count on knowing what's happening around town? When they hear the blare of that horrible siren, they feel part of a community—part of history."

Dick smiled. "I wouldn't go so far as to say that! Mrs. Knightly thinks the siren is keeping our city in the dark ages. But she, obviously, doesn't have your deep understanding of the whole situation," he added, smirking. "But that's not why she called. She wanted to know what I knew about the old hospital committee—you know, the one that was created years ago to dig up money to build the thing. She wanted to know who was on it."

"That was before my time. Shoot, I wasn't even working here then. It had to have been at least twenty years ago or so."

"Forty," Dick corrected him. "Even though I told her I'd try and find out what I could, I think I might just let it drop. I've got other things to do—more important things, than to look into something that doesn't even exist anymore."

"I think that's wise. No use wasting your time over something like that. I can ask Daisy what she knows, if you like. We should at least *try* to keep Mrs. Knightly happy."

"I think that would only happen if the siren broke."

They both had a good laugh then returned to their work. After all, it wouldn't do to have the public see them having fun on the city clock.

Jay waited for Dick to disappear down the hall and into his office. Then he hurried down the hall towards the mayor's office and quickly went inside. He opened the file cabinet that stood in the corner of the room and proceeded to thumb through the folders in search of the one marked *Hospital Minutes—1941*. There it was, in the back—not even in the correct alphabetical order.

He quickly opened it, only to find it was empty. The mayor must have taken it, he thought, just before he died. This could change everything.

CHAPTER TWELVE

Maggie kept herself busy over the next few weeks. Besides play practice, she had a piano recital to plan and students to prepare. She had also signed up to help with the school's fall festival. Not only was she supposed to bake three dozen cupcakes, she was supposed to work in the booth to sell them. Then, to top it all off, Wesley had come down with tonsillitis. Between doctor visits and staying up at night with him, she was finding it hard to make any extra time for herself.

In between the busyness of her life, Maggie's thoughts kept going back to Dolores and the hospital papers. She felt obligated to continue her investigation but wasn't sure she wanted to include Rob Stanger in it. Yes, it would be nice to compare notes with him, but she didn't like where things were going personally. She was relieved to see him immerse himself in the play each night. She was hopeful that he'd forget all about her in his pursuit of being the best Scrooge the town had ever seen.

It was on a Wednesday morning when Maggie saw the announcement in the newspaper. There, listed in the classified section, was a large ad about an open house in Trenton. Reading the address, she knew at once that Dolores's house was being sold. An idea suddenly came to her. She'd go to the open house and have another look around. Hopefully, she'd find some papers— important papers this time—that were more in keeping with what Dolores had told her about. If nothing turned up, well, then she'd know for sure that she'd done everything she possibly could. Only then could she stop feeling obligated towards Dolores and her mysterious papers.

Thursday morning, a bit later than planned, Maggie was parking her car on the side of the road past the familiar circular driveway. A white van advertising *Selma's Real Estate* was parked dominantly in the driveway, taking up the entire space. Maggie smiled to herself. Of course, Selma would be showing the house—who else? After all, she was the most sought-after realtor in town.

The house smelled like freshly-baked cookies when she entered. A young woman, wearing a lavender jacket, greeted her at the door. She handed her a brochure and told her to feel free to browse. Maggie thanked her then began 'browsing' her way down the basement stairs to have one more look through Dolores's broom closet.

She was excited to find a ladder in the corner, propped up against the cement wall—it hadn't been there before, or at least she hadn't seen it there before. She moved it into the broom closet and climbed to the top, this time determined to look before she touched to avoid any dead cockroaches. She saw an old can of motor oil on the top shelf, a few loose nails and a lot of dust, but no folder or papers of any kind. From her vantage point, she glanced around the room, especially at the tops of the other shelves but couldn't see anything. Disappointed, she started to climb down the ladder. Suddenly she was startled by a loud voice coming from behind.

"What are you doing up there!?"

The sudden interruption made Maggie jump, losing her hold on the ladder. Frantically, she tried to steady herself but to no avail.

"Whoa... careful there!"

Horrified, Maggie found herself falling off the ladder and into the arms of Brad Bennington.

As quickly as she could, she slid out of his grasp and tried to compose herself.

"Why, it's *you* again...the maid! What are you doing here in the basement?" Mr. Bennington's voice was demanding at first, but then softened a bit when he saw how upset she was. "Are you all right?"

Maggie's thoughts were going a mile a minute, trying to come up with a reason for being in the basement again. "My earring," she suddenly blurted out. "I lost my earring... the first time I was here. I thought this might be where I lost it, so I came to... to search for it." She realized she was stuttering.

He stared at her for a minute, trying to decide whether to believe her or not. "Well," he finally said, "did you find it?"

"No."

Brad Bennington looked at her suspiciously. "Well, come upstairs and have a cookie," he said, going against his usual nature and trying to show some hospitality. "Selma's in the kitchen baking some. She says the smell of cookies makes a house more saleable, for some reason or another. Maybe you'll find your earring there."

Maggie nodded, wanting nothing more than to get out of the basement and away from the embarrassing turn of events she'd gotten herself into again.

Brad led the way up the stairs. Midway, he paused. He slowly turned to look at Maggie.

"You sure you're okay?" he asked.

"Not a scratch, as they say." Maggie knew her voice sounded a bit shaky and hoped he hadn't noticed. She realized too, that he was staring at her most intently, making her feel even more uncomfortable.

"You're not married, are you? Or dating?"

He asked it so abruptly that it caught Maggie completely off guard, leaving her temporarily speechless. She quickly held up a shaky hand to show him her ring—the ring she hadn't been able to take off even though Hal had been gone for a year now.

"Oh, so you're married." Brad seemed disappointed.

"Not really, not anymore." Maggie quickly found her voice again.

"Divorced then?"

"No, widowed."

"Oh, I see," he replied, sounding strangely sympathetic. "In that case, would you consider going out with me sometime? Maybe dinner or something?"

Maggie was surprised. She decided he needed to hear the whole story. "Yes, I am widowed," she repeated, "with three children in tow."

"Ohhh…" Brad Bennington said the one word slowly, as if he needed a moment to assess the situation. "Never mind then," he added, ending the conversation as abruptly as he'd started it.

Maggie smiled and shook her head as she continued to follow him up the stairs. That was the easiest turn-down she'd ever had. She thought about the old saying of a bullet—dodging it and all—and decided she was very grateful, at least this time, for the dodge.

"Maggie! Maggie Brown!" Selma was enthusiastic when she saw Maggie emerge from the basement right behind Mr. Bennington. She rushed over to greet her, offering her one of the cookies. "I'm glad you decided to take me up on my offer to find you a house! When are you planning on moving back to Trenton?"

Maggie took one of the cookies, glad for a moment's diversion. Brad Bennington quickly ducked away through the back door, mumbling something about a rosebush that needed trimming in the backyard.

"I'm not sure yet—sure that I want to move back to Trenton, that is. I'm just exploring my options for now."

"Well, let me show you through the house. You're going to love it!" Selma eagerly began directing Maggie through each room. "It was built in the late sixties, so it's not really very old at all—relatively new, as a matter of fact. Notice the lovely furnishings. They all go with the house, you know. Everything does—the curtains, the wall-hangings, the appliances and furniture. They're all included. I see you have a brochure!" She pointed to the top of it where her name and phone number were prominently listed. "It's all there. Just give me a call when you decide, but don't leave it for too long if you want *this* house. I've already had three offers on it!"

As they passed through the hall to the living room, Maggie noticed a picture lying on one of the bookcases. In it, she saw Mayor Simple and Dolores along with two other people. She held the picture up for Selma to see.

"Who is this, here?" she asked, pointing to the other woman in the picture. "I've seen her before, at Dolores's funeral. She was talking to Brad Bennington."

"Oh, that's Mayor Simple's sister, Coralee. And I know this man standing next to her too!"

Selma pointed at the thin, tall man in the picture. He had dull black hair that fell heavily down his forehead. He was wearing a black suit, even though everyone else in the picture was dressed in light, summer clothes. He stood stiff and solemn, like a funeral director.

"That's the Simples' lawyer. Isn't he kind of creepy looking?"

Maggie had to agree.

"I saw him at Dolores's funeral," Selma continued. "I don't know why the Simple's would have a picture taken with him, do you? Oh well, I'm sure he's a nice guy underneath all the black!"

"I'm sure he is," Maggie said, with some reserve.

When the unwanted tour had finally come to an end, Selma led Maggie to the front room where her young assistant was posted. A middle-aged couple had just come in through the front door. Selma rushed over to greet them and immediately handed them one of her notorious brochures.

"Welcome to our open house!" she said brightly. "Please feel free to browse. I'll be with you in a minute to answer any questions you might have."

She turned to Maggie, impatient to end things now in order to catch up with the new, prospective clients. "Unless you have any more questions, I probably should be getting back to work."

"Just one more," Maggie said. "What happened to the desk that was in this room? I thought all the furniture went with the house."

The room in question was the one by the main entrance. She'd remembered the desk when she'd come before. It had had a lot of loose papers strewn upon it, and even more scattered across the floor.

"Yes, there was a desk—this room used to be the mayor's office. But it could be turned into a guest room instead, if you prefer," Selma advised. "With your three children, you'd probably want it as a bedroom though. A twin bed would fit fine in here, along with a nightstand. There would be plenty of room for toys too, if you put in some shelves. In fact, a shelf would look nice, just over here, and if you wanted to add more —perhaps a three-layer configuration over the bed? Whatever you think, I'm sure you can come up with some ideas on your own."

Maggie ignored Selma's decorating advice and asked, "But, what about the desk? I distinctly remember seeing it when I came before to visit Dolores."

"Sadly, it went somewhere else. I was hoping it would remain with the house—I had some plans for it myself—but the owner, Mr. Bennington, took it. As you've seen though, there are a lot of other fine pieces around, definitely worth something if you should decide to buy."

Maggie thanked Selma then turned to leave, hoping she wouldn't run into Brad Bennington outside. She quickly made her way to her car, content with what she'd tried to do today. *It was time to end this little mystery*, she thought, as she drove out of Trenton for the last time. She'd done everything humanly possible for Dolores and felt like she could now walk away from any further responsibility in the matter.

"That's funny," Selma's assistant remarked after Maggie had left. "She's the second person today to ask about that desk. Why would Mr. Bennington give it away to the mayor's sister, of all people? I met her at the funeral, you know—not a pleasant woman as far as I could tell. I can't recall her name though."

"Coralee," Selma answered. "Her name is Coralee Simple, and no—she isn't a pleasant woman by any means."

CHAPTER THIRTEEN

"Come down and meet your Aunt Sharlene and Uncle Dillon!" Maggie shouted up at Janie and Susan who were watching their guests arrive from the upstairs balcony. Susan hurried down the stairs as Janie sped by on the bannister. "And here's Sam and Kenny, your cousins!"

Susan quickly hid behind her mother, not sure about these strangers who'd come to her house.

"Uncle Dillon is my brother, you know. He lives far away in Michigan."

"Is that a long ways away?" Janie asked.

"Yes, a very long ways away!" Uncle Dillon answered as he smiled at the girls. He bent down to pick up Wesley who'd toddled over to see what was going on. "My, how he's grown! He looks a lot like his father!"

Maggie hugged her brother then took Wesley from him while he brought in the luggage.

"Smells like Thanksgiving around here!" Sharlene remarked as she took off her coat and hung it in the front closet. They all walked into the kitchen to get a close look at what was making the wonderful aromas.

"Why do you have a net in your backyard?" Sam and the other children had collected by the kitchen window, talking.

"That's Zachy's net," Susan told him.

"Who's Zachy and why does he have a net?" Kenny was curious.

"Zachy's our neighbor. He catches leaves in the net for us to jump in."

"That's stupid. I'd catch a cat, if I could. Or a dog. You could just throw that net over a dog or a cat and catch them easy."

"Why would you want to do that?" Susan said, thinking of Candy Corn all tangled up in Zachy's net. "That's even stupider than catching leaves!"

Dillon was circling the kitchen, surveying the holiday goodies crammed onto every available countertop and opening lids on pans to see what was inside. "Did you leave the potatoes for me?" he asked his mom.

"Of course, I did! I wouldn't dream of taking away your job. Thanksgiving traditions are important, as you know. It's so good to have you here, Dillon! It's been way too long!"

"We're glad it worked out that way. Sharlene has the book fair this Saturday and Sunday. Her boss has paid for the trip and for the time she'll spend there."

"Yes—our sister town, Mapleton, is sponsoring the international book fair this year. I've read all about it in the paper," Maggie commented. "Will you need to be there too, Dillon?"

"I'll probably wander around and look at some of the booths while Sharlene is working, but mostly, I'd like to spend time with you and the kids."

"Grandma, Kenny says our leaves are stupid!" Susan interrupted them.

"I did not! I said it's stupid to gather them in a net!"

"Now kids, let's get along. Janie, why don't you start putting the place markers on the table—the ones you and Susan helped make." Grandma was trying to be diplomatic. "Maybe Sam and Kenny would like to help."

"What will you be working on? At the book fair, I mean," Maggie asked Sharlene.

"I'll be looking over the rare manuscripts and books offered there. My boss would really like to get his hands on some early American literature—maps, transcripts, diaries—anything from that time period that I can find. You never know what will turn up at these fairs," Sharlene explained. "We have a lot of furniture come through our auction house, even toys and sports memorabilia. But my boss is keen to find some literature to add to our list. By the way, your mother was telling me that you've been playing the piano for the local theatre. What play are you doing?"

Maggie felt a bit overshadowed by the important job her sister-in-law had.

"Oh, yes. I'm spending time at the theatre now, behind the scenes, plunking my way through *A Christmas Carol*."

"The one Dickens wrote? I had no idea it was a musical," Sharlene seemed horrified at the prospect.

"Well, of course, Dickens didn't write it as a musical, but our director found one. I think it might've been written by one of her friends, or maybe even a relative."

"Oh, dear! Is it any good?"

"Not the best, no," Maggie said, then feeling a bit disloyal added, "but, not all that bad either. You'll have to come and see it. Opening night is Friday of next week."

"Wish we could stay that long, sis, but we have to be back on Monday morning," Dillon explained as he took the gravy bowl from his mother and sat it on the table.

"Now, all we need is someone to carve the turkey," Grandma announced as they assembled around the table in their assigned places. "It's so nice to have us all together again. All, that is, except our dear Hal and Grandpa. And since neither of them are here, will you do the honor, Dillon?" She placed the turkey platter in front of her son to carve.

Suddenly, the back door flew open and Candy Corn scampered in, followed by her owner.

"Sofie!" Maggie's mom exclaimed. "What brings you here today? Is something wrong—do you need our help?"

Sofie was carrying an empty measuring cup. "Sorry to disturb your meal," she said, "but could I borrow some sugar?"

In her gracious way, Maggie's mom took the measuring cup from Sofie and set it on the counter. "I'll get your sugar after we eat. Now, you sit down over there, by Janie. Maggie, get another plate out of the cupboard for Sofie."

Maggie was already a step ahead of her with the extra plate and silverware.

"You remember my son Dillon and his wife, Sharlene? And these two boys belong to him also—Sam and Kenny!"

"You'll really love it, Maggie. Books of all kinds are showcased—even music books. Dillon says he'll watch the kids so we can have the entire day to ourselves." Sharlene was coaxing Maggie to go with her to the book fair. "We can do lunch together too—my treat! C'mon, you've got to say yes!"

"I would really love to spend some time with you." Maggie tried to sound sincere but wasn't sure she really wanted to go. "You and Dillon have always lived so far away, ever since you were married. I finally have a sister but haven't been able to spend any time with her—with *you!* But I'd feel so out of place there."

"Now, that's just plain silly. It's open to the public, you know. Besides, leaving Dillon to deal with the kids on his own will do him good! He'd rather stay behind and visit with your mom anyway, so what do you say? Please come!"

Maggie decided to give in. "Well, why not—since you put it that way. But, shouldn't I change first? What does one wear to a book fair?"

"Exactly what you've go on, that's what!" Maggie's fashionable sister-in-law exclaimed as she walked out the door wearing her designer boots and coat."

Maggie put on her best coat over the jeans and pullover she was wearing then quickly added a scarf, as an afterthought, before following her sister-in-law out the door.

The International Antiquarian Book and Rare Manuscript Fair was held just outside Springville in the Mapleton Convention Center. The large, round building held hundreds of display booths. You could expect to find anything from Civil War books, railroad histories, rare maps on early colonization, musical manuscripts—there was even a booth on early whaling practices. The most popular booth seemed to be the one that advertised 'Free Appraisals'. It had the longest line of people in front of it.

"My boss has given me a budget," Sharlene explained. "He wants at least half a dozen antique books or maps to present at our auction house this spring. I'm just going to browse around and see what's available. You might like looking through the music, just over there. We can meet up at the south entrance at noon to go to lunch. I should be through by then."

"I don't mind tagging along with you. I can look at the music later," Maggie suggested.

"You'd be bored out of your mind! Really, feel free to browse through the booths that interest you. We'll have plenty of time to be together afterwards, during lunch."

Maggie watched as Sharlene hurried away towards the Civil War manuscript booth. Left standing alone in the vast building, she couldn't help but think it was strange that Sharlene had wanted to separate. Wasn't the whole idea of this outing to get to know each other better? How was that going to happen if they split up?

"Excuse me, but aren't you Maggie Brown?"

Maggie turned to see a slightly familiar face in front of her.

"Hi, I'm Maryanne Iverson. I met you at Dolores Simple's funeral—in the kitchen. I was one of the ladies helping with the food," she explained, introducing herself.

Maggie's mind went back to the scene at the church house. "Oh, yes! I remember you. It's nice to see you again."

Maryanne seemed pleased at being recognized. "I've been waiting for my husband to come and I noticed you standing here, all alone, so I thought I'd come and say hi."

"That's really nice of you. And it was nice meeting you at Dolores's funeral." Maggie realized how lame she sounded but Maryanne didn't seem to notice. She kept right on talking, obviously wanting something to do while she waited for her husband to come.

"Oh, yes. I'm afraid we didn't make a very good impression on you that day, in the kitchen, with all the gossiping that went on." Maryanne said.

Maggie smiled. "Oh, you don't have to worry about that! Remember, I used to live there—was part of the ladies' group —so I already knew what to expect. You must be a newcomer. Don't worry, you'll get used to their gossiping! They really mean no harm."

Maryanne Iverson smiled back, relieved. "Still, with all the talk about Dolores committing suicide, I didn't want you to get the wrong impression."

"What do you mean, wrong impression?" Maggie was confused.

"Well, that Dolores had actually *wanted* to take her own life. Because I know differently."

Maggie waited for her to proceed then realized a bit of prompting was called for. "*Why* do you know differently? Had Dolores said something to you?"

"Oh, no. Dolores and I weren't really friends. It's just that my cousin, Daisy Armstrong—you know, the receptionist at the city offices? Well, she told me about the flu shots that day. Why would Dolores get a flu shot if she had plans to... to do herself in? It really doesn't make any sense."

Maggie immediately thought it was Maryanne who wasn't making any sense here. "So, your cousin Daisy told you this? How did she know about Dolores getting a flu shot?"

"Because she was there, on that very day! They were giving flu shots at the city offices—some health program for all the city employees and their families—and Dolores Simple was there too, getting hers. Then, only minutes later, she ran her car off the bridge! Well, as you can see, it had to have been an accident. Why would she go to all the bother of getting a flu shot if she wasn't planning on living anymore?"

Maggie thought about it. "So, it must've been an accident, just like the police reported? That's good to know."

"Yes, it is good to know. And, as you can see, there's no truth in any of the gossiping that you might have heard."

Maggie couldn't help but think there might be another reason for Dolores's death that day. It was the reason suggested by Dolores herself when Maggie had gone to visit. The possibility of murder was still out there, even if it was unproven. Maggie entertained the idea only for a moment before dismissing it from her mind. *No use going there again*, she thought. That door had been closed once and for all, as far as she was concerned. No use opening it up again.

"There's my husband now, just coming in," Maryanne stated. "He's been looking forward to this convention for a long time. A big history buff, he is! I'll probably spend the rest of my time looking at old maps or something. Still, it's a day off, so who am I to complain? See you around!"

Maggie, alone again and still without a purpose, made her way to the music section to kill some time there. She found some old copies of Mendelssohn and Rubenstein that looked interesting but was disappointed when she discovered that the manuscripts weren't originals but early 'urtext' editions. She also found some publications of the Mary Magdalena Bach Notebook.

Again, not original—it would be highly unlikely to find an original of this compilation of pieces from the seventeenth century—but interesting, nonetheless.

"Could I help you, ma'am?" The salesman in the booth had made his way over to her. He looked as antiquated as the music he was offering. "I've noticed you looking at the Bach pieces. Would you be interested in knowing more about them?"

Maggie spent the next hour or so listening to the old man ramble on about the musical treasures he had to offer at the booth. There was even a piano there that he used to play the pieces for her.

Of course, she was familiar with each one and could have played them better herself but listened politely all the same, knowing she needed something to keep her busy until noon.

When the private recital was finally over, Maggie thanked the old man for his time then ventured out, once again, through the convention center. She'd gotten half-way across the room when, suddenly, something familiar caught her eye. It was a woman with a bright yellow scarf tied in her hair.

Maggie walked towards her, thinking this woman—at least from the back— looked a lot like Candy Turnbull, the librarian from Trenton. When she got closer, she could see that it *was* Miss Turnbull. Keeping her distance, she maneuvered herself into a position in order to watch her.

"I'm sorry, ma'am," Maggie overheard the man in the rare manuscript's booth respond to Miss Turnbull's question. "We haven't seen anything at all like you've described. I'd suggest that you check the Early American booth."

Maggie followed Miss Turnbull as she made her way to the next booth. "Sorry, we don't have anything like that in our collection," one of the saleswomen told her. "Perhaps we have something else that would interest you, though, if you care to look around. We have a lot to offer, like this diary from the civil war era, or maybe a roster of civilians who fought in the Revolutionary War?"

Candy Turnbull shook her head then moved on to the next booth, then the next, obviously looking for something specific. Maggie knew she was going to have to get closer if she was to hear what Miss Turnbull was asking for. Slowly and meticulously, she got in line just behind her.

Suddenly, Candy Turnbull turned and looked directly at her.

"Why, hello," Maggie said, trying to act casual. "You're the librarian from Trenton, right?"

Candy Turnbull looked Maggie squarely in the eyes. "And you're the woman who's been following me."

Maggie protested, stuttering, "I... I don't know what you mean."

"You were also at the library the other day, asking about Mayor Simple. What is it that you want from me? Do you know something?"

Maggie felt trapped, realizing she *knew* absolutely nothing when it got right down to it. Still, she felt like she needed to defend herself. "No, of course not—what a funny question. What would *I* know? I'm here at the book fair with my sister-in-law. It's just coincidence that we ran into each other, nothing else. But you seem to be looking for something specific. Can I help you find it?"

Candy gave Maggie a withering stare. "No, thank you," she stated emphatically, then walked away, disappearing into the crowd.

Maggie quickly made her way to the foyer to wait for Sharlene to come. More than ever she was wishing she hadn't come today. Just when she'd made up her mind to forget all about Dolores Simple's death and the mysterious papers surrounding it, she felt like she'd been put right back in the thick of it. Candy Turnbull must have been involved with the mayor after all, Maggie realized. There was no other explanation for her actions today. And the papers Dolores had told her about must still be out there as a silent clue to the whole mess.

"Maggie, you're right on time!" Sharlene suddenly came up from behind, carrying some old books and folders in her arms. "Are you ready for lunch? I certainly am. And you won't believe the luck I've had today. My boss will be so pleased when he sees what I've found!"

CHAPTER FOURTEEN

"How's the investigation going?"

Maggie and her mom were driving home from the airport after seeing Dillon and his family off. The kids were asleep in the back seat and, typically, Mom was asking a lot of questions.

"I wouldn't call it an investigation. Nothing is really happening—at least, not much."

"Now, you don't know that for sure. Things might be happening, and you just don't know. Start at the beginning and tell me everything you've found. Maybe I can help you sort them out."

"Mom, do we have to do this? I'm really tired."

"All the more reason to talk. I don't want you falling asleep at the wheel." Maggie's mom always had a point. "Have you found out anything about the hospital minutes—who the contributors were and why Dolores hid them in her closet?"

"That's just it, Mom. I don't think those minutes mean anything after all. I think Dolores was—well, she had more than her share of nervous exhaustion during that time. And rightly so, considering she'd just lost her husband."

"Okay, so that's what you've decided—that Dolores was delirious? How about we just deal with the facts—the tangible things that really happened and not mere speculation. Start with the funeral. Did you find anything significant there?"

Maggie realized her mom wasn't going to drop the subject no matter how much she tried to avoid it. This was like a game to her, so she decided to give in and play along.

"There was some gossip about Mayor Simple having an affair with a woman named Candy Turnbull. She's the new librarian in town."

"Really? Do you think there was anything to it?"

"I wouldn't have thought so, but after seeing her at the book fair…"

"The librarian was at the book fair!? What was she doing there?"

"A librarian at a book fair? Really, Mom?"

Her mom ignored the cynicism. "Your tone of voice leads me to believe that there was some significance in her being there—library duties aside. Besides, I very much doubt she'd be there to purchase anything. Those books cost a lot of money! Much more than a local library could afford."

"Especially *that* library. They seem to be having some financial issues that the city council is unwilling to help with. But yes—the thought *did* cross my mind that Candy Turnbull was there looking for something. Perhaps she was trying to locate the mysterious papers that Dolores Simple told me about."

"I rather doubt it. We already know what those are—you have them in a folder in your room!"

"That's just the point, Mom. I don't think the papers we have are the right ones. If we're going to pursue this case—

which I don't think we should, by the way—but, if we do, we're going to have to look elsewhere."

"Maybe you need to go back to Dolores's house and look again."

Maggie was silent for a moment, not sure she wanted to tell her mother that she'd done just that—looked for the papers a second time in Dolores's basement. But before she could say anything more on the subject, her mother had moved onto a new line of questioning.

"So, what else have you been doing, Maggie? You seem to be spending a lot of time with that man—Rob, is it? The one who met you on the back porch the night of Halloween?"

Maggie bristled. It was just like her mother to go from the frying pan directly into the fire.

"He's just an actor in the play—Scrooge, as a matter of fact. He's doing some investigating too."

"Oh, is he a policeman? Or a detective?"

"No, Mom. He teaches law at the university but does some private investigating on the side."

"Really?" The word was drawn out, spoken with renewed interest. Maggie's mom was beginning to think that this actor was someone she should start taking seriously—someone whom Maggie should start taking seriously. "Just what is he investigating?"

"It seems he's trying to find some missing papers too. I ran into him at the Trenton City Library a few weeks ago." Maggie laughed. "For a moment, I actually thought you might've hired him."

"Why would you think that? That's just plain silly, dear."

"Because you're always trying to get me out of the house to date."

"But I don't even know him!"

"I know. I was just overthinking it, as usual."

"Well, what did he want? I mean, when you met on the porch that night."

"He said we should join forces—his words, not mine—to find the papers."

"Did you show him what you'd found?"

"Yes, but he didn't seem to think they were of any consequence. Neither do I now."

"You know, it occurs to me that this Rob is more interested in you than in any papers he's looking for. Even so, he's taking this investigation a lot more seriously than you are. Do you think he's actively looking for a murderer as well?"

"Really, Mom? We don't even know if a murder has been committed! In fact, this whole thing has just been a game for us!"

"Rob seems to think it's more than just a game!"

Maggie decided to give up. "Perhaps it's more than just a game," she said, "and perhaps Dolores and her husband *were* murdered. I guess it won't hurt for us to keep our eyes open and see what we can find."

"I think you're going to need to do more than just 'see what you find'. If you're going to do this thing—be involved in this investigation—then you're going to have to be a bit bolder. Are you keeping a list of clues? Writing down the important and even unimportant things in a notebook can prove to be very valuable. That way, you can see what they have in common, or what they don't have in common—what is relevant and what is irrelevant."

"Mom, I don't have time for that! Besides, everything is so complicated. How would I even begin to know what's relevant?"

"The important clues will rise to the top of the list, eventually, in a simple yet direct way, and the rest will fall away. That's how."

"And, how do you know that? Miss Marple, I presume? You know that's fiction, don't you? Well, this is real life and I don't want to get mixed up in anything too risky!"

Maggie's mom sighed. "I don't mean you should do anything dangerous, but you could try to be more—well… more of a snoop! That's how you find things out, you know."

Maggie started to laugh, realizing her mother was taking this so-called investigation way outside the realms of reality. "Maybe I can take lessons from the church ladies in Trenton. They seem to be well-versed on all things snoopy. Anyway, we're here."

Maggie had never been so relieved to be pulling the car into the driveway.

CHAPTER FIFTEEN

Snow had finally come to the small town of Springville. It had come in the night, secretly and softly, leaving a thin blanket of white to cover the ground. Everyone was getting in the Christmas spirit and with the arrival of snow, enchantment was in the air. Downtown shoppers hurried in and out of the shops, hoping to find just the right gifts for the people on their lists.

Choirs began to prepare for cantatas, fir trees were brought home to decorate, lights were hung, baked goods were made, and children everywhere were making lists for Santa.

The period costumes Mrs. Barker had collected for the play were becoming part of the seasonal charm too. Dicken's England was brought to life as top hats, waistcoats, capes and canes were donned by the men and long skirts, lacey blouses, and bonnets by the women. Mr. Benson was proving his worth at painting background scenes, making the illusion of a nineteenth century Christmas appear upon the walls of the old barn. All the necessary elements were in place for the magic of the theatre to blend with the magic of the season.

A small orchestra, hand-picked by Mrs. Barker herself, was set to practice tonight exactly one hour before the actors were to arrive. Mrs. Barker welcomed them then introduced each member to the group.

"Our drummer, Dale Redding—nice to have you, Dale— is sitting next to our violinists, Julie Newton, Laura Blanchard, and Kylie Dunlap. Ladies, we should move you to my right, next to Anson Thompson and his bass over here. That's the ticket," she paused, waiting for them to move before continuing. "Melissa and Karen are our flutists, and Kelton, Weston, Henry, and Gary are our brass section." She smiled at the six high school band students seated together on the back row away from the adults. "And, of course, their very own band teacher, Mr. Wilson, is our clarinetist—then Sue Williams on the cello and Maggie Brown at the piano."

"Did I have the time for the practice wrong?" Maggie spoke up, a bit confused as to why she'd arrived so much earlier than the others.

Dale Redding jumped in with the answer before Mrs. Barker could reply. "Trudy has a habit of setting our practice time earlier than it actually is, in hopes we'll eventually arrive."

"Musicians," Mrs. Barker said the word condescendingly. "Musicians have no sense of time, dear, only of meter. Now, quickly get out your music. We have only one hour to rehearse before the actors join us for the final dress rehearsal."

Dale Redding gave Maggie a quick wink. She smiled back, trying not to look too irritated at having a half-hour of her own time wasted over not understanding 'musician time'.

Mrs. Barker led them through the score, stopping only briefly to work out wrong notes or tempos or to show them where the cuts were. Most of the musicians came prepared for alterations and had brought their own pencils. For those unprepared, Mrs. Barker had extras and passed them out liberally.

By the end of the rehearsal, Maggie had started to warm up to the small group. She was surprised at how they all worked together, even the high school kids.

Mrs. Barker was pleased too. "Very nice! You're all marvelous!" she complimented them generously. "Let's break for fifteen minutes now, then we'll do it all over again, next time with the actors!"

"Does that mean fifteen minutes 'musician time'?" Maggie asked Dale Redding as the group walked out of the orchestra pit towards the lobby.

Dale quickly fell in step alongside her. "I think, this time, she really means what she says. Hey, you really know your way around the keyboard. Maybe I'll send my boys to you for some piano lessons. I hear you're teaching over at your mom's house."

"Yes, I've been living with her for a year now—ever since my husband... *died*." Maggie still couldn't get used to saying the word aloud.

"Did you know, I used to work at the *Trenton Daily Reporter* with him? Hal was a great guy. I was sorry to hear of his passing."

"Really? You worked with him?" Maggie was surprised. "How long ago was that?"

"Well, let's see—I got the job with the *Springville Examiner* two years ago last fall. I worked at the *Trenton Daily* up until then, with Hal."

"So, you're a reporter?"

Dale laughed. "Sometimes. I mostly work as an editor now. I used to work exclusively as a reporter back then, in the Trenton days. Would you like a soda? No cost to us musicians, you know."

They'd stopped in front of the concession stand. A few other people, mostly friends and relatives of the cast, had started to arrive to watch the dress rehearsal. Dale asked the girl behind the counter for two sodas.

"My wife and kids should be coming in anytime now," Dale continued. "Do you have anyone coming tonight?"

"No, not tonight, but my mom's planning on bringing the kids on Saturday."

"How many kids do you have? I remember two girls...?"

"Add a baby boy to that and you've got it right. We have three of them—or, at least, *I* have three. Hal died the same night the baby came, during that crazy snowstorm last winter."

Dale looked at Maggie with concern, hoping he wasn't digging up too many sad memories for her. "You know," he said, "Hal was a great guy to work with. He was a fantastic reporter—even had some topics he kept on file, waiting for them to come to full fruition. He was patient enough to wait for the stories to unfold—collecting evidence all the time, you see —even if it took months to make sure all the elements of the story were there before making his final report. He was a stickler for getting the facts right!"

Maggie listened intently. For the first time since Hal had died, she was able to talk about him. It felt good, and she told Dale how much she appreciated his words.

"Yes, Hal was a great reporter and a good man as well. I was lucky to have known him." Dale looked up, his smile broadening. "Why, here's Stacy and the kids now, just coming in! I'd love for you to come meet them."

Dale was obviously very proud of his little family. Maggie smiled as he introduced his wife and their two boys to her.

"Well, we'd better be getting back to the orchestra pit—it's almost time for the overture to begin," Dale announced, looking at his wristwatch. "If you sit on the right side, you can see the play the best," he instructed his wife as he ushered her and the kids into the theatre.

Maggie felt a mix of emotions swelling up in her as she walked back to the orchestra pit, mostly nervousness for the dress rehearsal but also a bit of loneliness mixed in. She realized that seeing Dale with his wife had brought it on. They appeared to be so happy together. It wasn't that she was jealous of them, she just missed Hal. She wished, for a moment, that he could be with her tonight but then pushed it out of her mind to concentrate on the play.

She spotted Rob Stanger from across the room, looking out of the curtain in the back, and felt a pang of guilt. First loneliness, then guilt. She felt like she couldn't win. How long would it take before she could stop thinking about Hal and be able to move on to someone else?

The overture began, right on time, and she immersed herself in the music. Soon, the lights came up on the stage and the cold, stark office of Ebenezer Scrooge came to life. Out of nowhere, the chilling voice of the narrator spoke.

"Old Marley was as dead as a door nail…"

Mrs. Barker was perched on a stool next to the piano, listening to the narrator recite the opening lines. "I've told him a million times *not* to emphasize 'door nail'," she whispered to Maggie, then continued to fume as the first scene unfolded layer by layer. Nervously, she kept moving from the stool to the curtain then back again. Maggie counted three times during the first half of the play when she left the orchestra pit altogether to sit with the audience. But, even then she was back on cue and ready to conduct the music when needed.

Maggie noticed that two of the high school boys—Henry and Gary—had earphones on—tiny white dots connected to two white cords—plugged into a small radio next to them. She watched as Mr. Wilson, their teacher, pointed to them and shook his head. One of the boys mouthed the words '*It's the ballgame*', to which Mr. Wilson gave them a thumbs-up and whispered, '*What's the score*'?

Laura Blanchard, one of the violinists, looked at the boys in disgust then whispered something to the other violinists who immediately shook their heads in agreement.

Anson, the bass player, kept twirling his big bass back and forth on its endpin to pass the time between the musical numbers, making Julie Newton scoot her chair forward to avoid being hit.

All sorts of things Maggie never imagined seemed to be happening in the pit. Only a few of the musicians were actually listening to the play on the other side of the curtain. But when Mrs. Barker hurried to the front, ready to direct them in the next musical number, they would all spring to attention, ready to play.

When Fezziwig's scene was upon them, Laura Blanchard sat forward in her chair, ready to play the solo of the lone fiddler dancing his way across the stage. It was a Christmas party from Scrooge's past, and the merry tune of the fiddler soon changed into a lively dance with everyone joining in. This was Maggie's favorite scene. The music was as fun to play as it was to listen to.

She thought how great it would be to dance to it and envied the actors on stage.

The play continued until Scrooge had encountered all three ghosts, one at a time. When they'd all left, he was alone in his bedroom. Realizing it was Christmas Day, he suddenly became giddy with delight. He was now a changed man and Rob Stanger, keeping in character, was making the most of it.

"He's so good in this part," Mrs. Barker whispered to Maggie. "In fact, he's the best Scrooge I've ever had."

"He's good, all right," Maggie had to admit.

"A good man too," Mrs. Barker continued. "Ever since his wife passed away—oh, it's been about three years now—he's been with us, playing the part of Scrooge."

"His wife?" Maggie started to ask, but Mrs. Barker had already jumped up to lead the music for the curtain call. On stage, the actors and actresses were dancing their way into a collective bow, responding to the enthusiastic applause from the audience. Mrs. Barker, overly pleased at their response and obviously high on adrenaline, was leading the music much too fast. Maggie was having a hard time keeping up with the tempo, and it didn't help that her mind was on other things. Why had Rob not told her about his wife?

"You still can't be walking home, not after the last snowfall!" Rob had caught up with Maggie just outside the old barn after the play had ended. "You've got to let me drive you home now, for sure."

Maggie paused, trying to decide.

"You wait here, just inside the lobby. I'll warm up the jeep and be right back for you." Rob sprinted off towards the parking lot before Maggie could protest further.

Minutes later, the jeep pulled up and Maggie got inside. Just as Rob had said, it was nice and warm.

"How about we take a detour and look at all the Christmas lights around town?" Rob suggested, clearly not wanting the night to end.

"I probably should get home to the kids."

"They'll be asleep by now, and twenty more minutes won't hurt. Besides, I'm much too wired to go home yet—I always am after a performance." He drove on past her house.

"How's your investigation going?" Maggie casually asked, curious to hear if he had found anything pertinent.

"There's not a lot happening there. Has Mrs. Knightly found anything for you—about the hospital minutes you have?"

"No, and she probably won't either. Those minutes are just not important at all, like you said on the night you looked them over. But, what kind of papers are *you* looking for?"

"I'm really not sure, if truth be told. Yes, I was hired to find some, but the papers you showed me, well, I agree with you— they're not worth anything. Like Mrs. Knightly said, the committee was disbanded long ago when a large company stepped in to take over the building of the hospital, so nothing even became of the plans that were written in those minutes. At least, that's the way I see it."

"But you continue to look for other papers of value. Now, remind me. Who did you say hired you to look for them?"

Rob laughed. "Nice try, Maggie. You know I can't tell you that. Besides, what good would it do if you knew?"

"Probably none at all," Maggie conceded. "By the way, your performance was really good tonight. Mrs. Barker even said so."

"Well, there you have it—straight from the horse's mouth!"

Maggie laughed. "I've never heard Mrs. Barker compared to a horse before—or were you talking about me?!"

"Now, would I compare either of you to a horse? Seriously though, I've been playing the part of Scrooge for years. I should know how to do it by now."

"So, I've heard. Mrs. Barker said you've been doing it ever since your wife died."

Suddenly, there was a deep silence inside the jeep. All Maggie could hear was the low humming of the motor and the faint sound of Christmas music filtering in from the town square.

Finally, Rob spoke.

"We were married four years ago, in the spring. By fall, she was gone. Cancer." He spoke hesitantly, as if the words still had power to hurt.

"I'm so sorry," Maggie said, wishing now she hadn't brought it up. "Mrs. Barker just mentioned it—that you'd been married—and I, well...I didn't know, you see. I didn't know about your wife—about you being married before, and about her illness. I really am sorry..." Maggie knew she was babbling but couldn't seem to find the right words.

"Don't be sorry," Rob said. "It was something I probably should have mentioned to you before. Besides, the years have helped me get over it, in a way. Time and work—lots of work. I finished law school after she died then began working at the university. When that wasn't enough, I got my license to work as a private detective. Still, it left me time to think, so I started doing plays at the old barn. Finally, I was able to keep myself so busy that I could fall asleep at night."

Maggie put her hand on his arm. "I am so sorry. I had no idea."

Rob pulled the jeep over to the curb. The Christmas lights from the town square shown lightly through the window of the jeep. "You lost your husband too, not so long ago. I should be sorry for you."

"No, no," Maggie protested. "I've been very lonely, it's true, but I have the kids to keep me busy. That makes a big difference."

Rob turned in his seat to face her. Maggie thought how nice he looked—very handsome with his dark eyes looking at her so seriously. Not as handsome as Hal though. She quickly looked away, immediately regretting the comparison. He turned her face back towards his, gently. Then he put his arms around her and kissed her.

After what seemed to be a long silence, Maggie turned away, confused. "I'm… I'm sorry…" she whispered.

"You seem to be sorry a lot," Rob said, disappointedly. "I just thought… assumed… that you liked me."

Maggie was confused. "No, it's not that. I *do* like you."

"Then what's the problem? No, don't tell me. You think it's too soon. Is that it?"

Maggie looked at Rob, surprised he knew her thoughts. But then, of course he would. He'd been through the same process when he lost his wife.

"I don't know why I can't move on," she blurted out. "It's been a year now—well, almost, and it still feels like I'm… like I'm…"

"Cheating." Rob finished the sentence for her. "It feels like you're cheating. Believe me, I know! It took me over a year to stop feeling that way."

"I'm so relieved you understand. You don't know how much it means to me."

"So, I should probably take you home now?" His voice had become softer as he waited patiently for her answer.

"Yes, it's probably the best thing to do. Perhaps we can see the lights another time."

Rob turned the jeep back onto the road and drove Maggie home, wishing all the time that he hadn't rushed things with her tonight. If she needed more time, then she should have it. After all, he had all the time in the world.

Chapter Sixteen

"…Eight maids a-milking, seven swans a-swimming, six geese a-laying…five gold-en rings. Four calling birds, three French hens, two turtle doves, and a partridge in a pear tree."

Maggie was singing at the top of her lungs as Janie and Susan acted out the words of her song. Even Wesley, sitting in his highchair and eating some of Grandma's Christmas cookies, was entertained by the broad antics his mother and sisters were displaying. It was Saturday morning, and Grandma was out shopping. Maggie was enjoying having the extra time alone with her kids.

Before she could move on to the ninth day of Christmas, the doorbell rang, interrupting them. She quickly wiped the cookies off Wesley's hands and mouth then picked him up before hurrying to the front door to answer it. Janie and Susan followed right behind.

Two men, dressed in suits, were standing on the porch. Maggie opened the door but didn't invite them in.

"Are you Maggie Brown?" the older one asked. He was heavy set and wore a grey suit that matched his hair. The younger one wore a black suit and was tall and thin.

"Yes, I am. Who are you?" They looked harmless enough, but Maggie wasn't going to ask them in until she knew what they wanted and who they were.

"I'm Detective Jake Milton and this is my partner, Russ Secrist." He showed her his badge.

"Can we talk to you?"

Maggie still didn't budge, except to adjust Wesley on her hip. "What do you need to talk to me about?" she asked.

"We're investigating the murder of Coralee Simple and we understand that you knew her brother and sister-in-law, Greg and Dolores Simple."

Maggie was stunned. She hadn't expected *this*. "Yes, I know, or at least *knew* the Simples, but I didn't know Coralee. I've heard her name spoken, briefly, by my friend Selma Wright. She's a realtor in Trenton."

"Well, Coralee was Greg's sister, as I said. Dolores's brother, Brad Bennington, told us you were Dolores Simple's maid and that you might also know Coralee Simple. Apparently, she was in their house, looking around after Dolores's death. Brad said you were in the house at the time, cleaning. Were you in the Simples' house at that time?"

"Why, yes. I guess I was."

"And did you notice anything unusual? Anything that might help us with our investigation?"

Maggie opened the door wider to let them in. "I think you'd better come in and sit down. Janie, Susan, run upstairs and play in your room for a while. I'll come and get you in a minute."

When they were all seated in the parlor, Maggie began to explain.

"I'm not really Dolores's maid. I just wanted to help, so I went that day, after she died, to clean her house."

"Yes, go on." Detective Secrist was writing her words down in a little notebook.

"Well, I'd visited Dolores the day before her accident and she'd told me where to find some papers if she—well, I know how crazy this sounds, but if she *died*. She thought someone was trying to kill her and I was led to believe it was because of the papers she'd told me about."

"That's interesting. Did you find any papers that day?" Detective Milton asked.

"Yes, I did. I'll go and get them for you, if you'd like."

"Yes, I think that would be a good idea."

Maggie hurried upstairs to get the blue folder from her dresser drawer, checking in on the girls as she did. Then she walked back down slowly, trying to compose herself, hoping that Detective Milton wouldn't think she was a thief.

"I wouldn't have taken these if Dolores hadn't told me to, you know," she said as she handed the folder to Milton who opened it immediately and carefully looked through its contents.

"Why, these are just some random minutes from a meeting." He glanced at the first page again, "held decades ago. Why would Dolores want you to take them?"

"She was a bit odd at the time. I thought it was because she'd just lost her husband. I couldn't see how the minutes from a hospital meeting could be that important either. Are they?"

"Absolutely not! These are worthless, as far as I'm concerned. Maybe an historian might find them useful, but even then, I doubt it. He started to hand the folder back to Maggie then hesitated. "Still, perhaps I should keep them— have them looked over properly at headquarters."

He handed them to Detective Secrist instead.

"Is there anything else you'd like to tell us about Coralee Simple, while we're here?" Detective Milton asked.

"Like I said before, I didn't really know her. I thought I was alone in the house, the day I went to clean. Well, except for Brad Bennington. He was there when I arrived."

Detective Milton produced a snapshot from his coat pocket and held it up for Maggie to see.

"Have you ever seen this man before?" he asked.

Maggie looked at the picture and immediately recognized the strange-looking man in the photo.

"That's the Simple's lawyer, or so I've been told."

"Their lawyer…hmmm. This is Coralee's ex-husband— well, one of them. The third, to be exact. His name is Malcolm Graves. Why did you think he was their lawyer?"

"My friend, Selma, pointed him out to me and told me he was their lawyer. She said she saw him at Dolores's funeral. Why? Is he a suspect?" she asked, curiously.

"I really can't say at this point," Detective Milton said. Perhaps we need to talk with this Selma. What did you say her last name was?"

"Selma Wright. She owns and operates Selma's Real Estate in Trenton."

Maggie saw Detective Milton writing it all down in his notebook.

"Well, thanks for your cooperation," Milton said, ready to leave. "Here's my number."

He stood, handing Maggie his card. "If you think of anything else that might be of importance, I'd appreciate a call."

Maggie walked them to the door. "Do you mind telling me how this Miss Simple died?" she asked, taking her mother's advice on being snoopy. She felt odd asking, as it was really none of her business.

Detective Secrist took out a snapshot from his coat pocket and handed it to Maggie. It showed a woman, lying on the floor next to a large mahogany desk, her head covered in blood.

Maggie shuddered. "Why, that's the lady in the hall, at the funeral!" she exclaimed.

"Which funeral? Which hall?" Detective Milton was keen to find out more.

"At Dolores's funeral. She was arguing with Brad Bennington in the hall at the church house."

"And, just what was it they were arguing about?" Detective Secrist opened his notepad and clicked on his pen again, ready to record her words.

Maggie thought for a minute, trying to remember the conversation she'd overheard that day as she'd hid in the ladies' room at the church house. "They were arguing about papers," she said, "and a desk that had been in her family for years!"

She looked at the snapshot once again—at the poor victim lying against the respectable, old desk—then quickly handed it back to Detective Secrist.

"Is Rob Stanger here?" Maggie asked the student sitting at the booth marked *Criminal Law*.

Rob had told her last night at the play that he would be working his University job fair the following afternoon.

"He had to get something from his office," the college girl replied nonchalantly, smacking her gum and making it pop. "He'll be right back."

"What's his room number? I'll catch up with him there."

"It's 416. But, if you go to his room, you might pass him coming back down in the elevator. You'd be better off waiting here."

Maggie was too nervous to just sit and wait. "I'll take my chances," she said, hurrying off towards the elevators. She needed to find Rob as quickly as possible and tell him about Coralee's murder and the possible significance it had in the deaths of Dolores and the Mayor.

She was hoping Rob could help her make sense of it all.

The elevator dinged and Maggie got off on the third floor. She walked down the deserted hall, watching the room numbers get larger as she did. There, at the end, was room 416. Its open door faced her and as she got closer, she could hear voices coming from inside. Rob was there, talking to someone.

"The librarian, Candy Turnbull. Did you find anything when you spoke with her?" Maggie heard someone ask. His voice sounded familiar. She stopped to wait behind the door, not wanting to interrupt them.

"It was interesting." Maggie heard Rob speak next. "She was very defensive when I suggested she knew Mayor Simple, but then started to ask if I knew anything about the papers he had, so she obviously knew him well enough to know he had them. When I tried to get her to tell me what she knew, she just stopped talking. Didn't say another word the whole time."

"So, she doesn't have them. What about that other lead? You said you knew someone else who'd taken papers from Dolores's house. What happened with that?"

"Oh, yes," Maggie heard Rob laugh. "That proved to be a dead-end too. She showed me a folder that contained minutes to a hospital meeting. Obviously, Dolores had led her to believe they were important. Poor girl—she was led on a wild goose chase!" Rob chuckled again.

"Who was that girl? What's her name?"

"Her name's Maggie Brown. She plays piano for the play."

"I know who you're talking about. She's the girl who came to Dolores's house to clean—a widow with three children." His voice sounded decidedly flat. "I got her name from the ladies in the kitchen, the day of the funeral. I told Detective Milton to check up on her. Maybe she knows more than she's telling."

"What do you mean, you got Detective Milton to check up on her? Has she done something?"

"Possibly. All I know is that she was snooping around Dolores's house—twice, actually, pretending to be the maid."

"Seriously, Brad. She's nothing. You need to leave her alone."

"Oh, I definitely plan on leaving her alone! She's nice looking and all, but three children? I'm not touching that with a ten-foot pole! I'll leave her to the police and see what they find."

Horrified, Maggie held her breath, listening carefully to hear what they were saying. She couldn't believe that anyone, even someone as callous as Brad Bennington, would think her capable of any wrongdoing.

Rob voiced what Maggie was thinking. "Brad, you're not making any sense! Why would the police even be interested in Maggie Brown? What are you getting at?"

"Coralee Simple's recent murder—that's what. She was pushed hard against that darn mahogany desk she so adamantly demanded I turn over to her—hit her head and died. Now, I'm not saying this Maggie Brown did it, but somebody did, and it could've been her."

Maggie wedged herself between the wall and the open door to keep from being seen. She couldn't believe what she was hearing.

"This is a very interesting turn of events," she heard Rob say. "Do you think Coralee's murder could be related to the papers we've been looking for?"

"Of course, it is. She's been looking for those papers too, you know. Why else would she want the desk? She thought she'd find the papers in it, that's why. But I turned it out thoroughly before I let her have it—there was nothing left there to find!"

"So, you think whoever murdered her did so to get his hands on the papers?"

"That's exactly what I'm saying."

"Hmm. Sounds about right, I guess. But that alone rules out Maggie Brown. She's not looking for any papers—she thinks she already has the ones Dolores was talking about."

"Does she own a woolen scarf?"

"What do you mean? Everyone in this part of the country owns a woolen scarf!"

"Forensics found woolen fibers under Coralee's fingernails —green, in fact. And, since Coralee wasn't wearing anything woolen when she died, they figured she had grabbed onto something that the murderer had on."

"And how do you know that?" Rob sounded skeptical.

"Oh, I know someone from the coroner's office." Brad sounded extra cocky. "He told me all about it, after some incentive."

Rob snorted. He understood well the type of incentive Brad would have given. "Well, I'm sorry to hear that Coralee Simple is dead," Rob said, "even though I didn't really know her. But, what's next? Do you still want me to look for the missing papers?"

"No, we need to let things lie dormant for a while, at least until this murder business blows over."

"I see. So, I stop looking for your precious papers for now? Okay, no problem. But I'll be sending you a bill for the time I've already spent on it."

"Send it if you like, but as far as I'm concerned, no papers, no money. I expect results before I pay anyone."

Maggie decided she'd heard enough. She hurried out of the building as fast as she could, wondering all the time the extent of Rob's involvement. She realized, in a way, that she was involved as well. She'd believed Dolores's story about the hidden papers, even to the point of masquerading as a maid to retrieve them from her broom closet—and all because Dolores had turned up dead herself, just like her husband.

CHAPTER SEVENTEEN

Trenton City Council consisted of four men: Terence Cole, Mike Sanders, Richard Gailey and Fred Hurst; and two women, Louise Holt and Sharon Brockman. Also attending the Council meetings were Jay Lindt, the city recorder, Rick Wood, the city manager, and the newly appointed pro-temp mayor, Fran Knightly. The meetings were held in the courtroom every Tuesday night at 7:00.

On the agenda tonight were discussions on the snow removal problem (the city crew had run out of road salt and needed more money), the Christmas decorations on Main (the citizens were complaining that they looked too modern and wanted the old ones back), the year-end financial report (which included the library funds) and, as usual, Mrs. Knightly wanted another vote to discontinue the town siren.

"It's outdated, noisy, and since the invention of pagers and telephones, totally unnecessary!" Mrs. Knightly stated her opinion forcefully—an opinion that each council member knew by heart.

"We know how you feel about it," Rick Wood spoke for the entire group. "But it has to remain. You know how the citizens of Trenton feel about it. They would be up in arms if we took it down. Look at how they responded to the new Christmas decorations! They just don't like change and we, as their representatives, need to take that into consideration. I move that we table this discussion and go on the next item on the agenda."

Terence Cole seconded the motion and Mrs. Knightly reluctantly conceded. "Let's move on to the financial report then," she stated.

"Before we do," Mike Sanders interrupted, "may I take a few minutes to finalize the plans for our Christmas party? First, I need a vote on who's coming."

Everyone raised their hands, everyone except Sharon Brockman.

"Sharon, you'll be missing out on a fine dinner," Mike said. "It's going to be catered by the Chalmer's Café and Doughnut Shop this year."

Sharon stood to give her reason for missing. "Dave's office party is scheduled for the same night—sorry."

"We understand, but, just so you know, you'll be missed! Now, we thought it would be nice to recognize our late mayor, Greg Simple, at the party. Something along the lines of a plaque or some sort of gift for his dedicated service to our community. "

"A plaque probably wouldn't work, seeing as how the mayor didn't have any children to pass it along to," Councilwoman Sharon noted. "And his wife Dolores just recently passed away too. Without anyone to accept the plaque —I just don't see how it would work."

"Perhaps Mrs. Knightly, as mayor pro-temp, could accept it," Dick suggested.

"We could have a plaque made up," Mrs. Knightly offered her idea on the subject, "then put it in the display cabinet in the foyer, as a memorial. I'll find out a bit about his life too, for a short article in the newspaper."

Mike made a motion to put Sharon in charge of ordering the plaque and Mrs. Knightly in charge of placing an article in the paper. Councilman Richard Gailey seconded it, and it was voted on unanimously.

"Now, I'd like to turn some time over to Miss Candy Turnbull, our librarian," Mrs. Knightly stated. "She is here to report on the library funds. Miss Turnbull."

Candy stood in front of the city council wearing her brightly colored signature head scarf and gave her report. She then went on to ask the council to approve funding for an addition to the library.

"The library is in desperate need of money, as you can see," she pleaded. "We need to keep up with our growing community and, although the Friends of the Library have collected some funds before they were dissolved, I'm asking you, as the city council, to authorize more—at least match what we've already collected."

"I hardly think a library is the right place, especially at this time, to put our meager funds towards. Being able to check out a book is hardly a *need,* Miss Turnbull," Mike Sanders put in his two-cents' worth.

"I have to agree with Mike," Richard Gailey also spoke, "I've never in my life *needed* to check out a book." There was some chuckling throughout the room. "Don't get me wrong, they're nice to have around—libraries—when you've got the time for them. But, surely, we have plenty of books already for that purpose. I don't think Trenton needs more. Our citizens should be happy with what we already offer."

"It's not just for books," Candy Turnbull tried to mask her frustration to explain further, "It's for computers too, and a new children's section. And, of course, an addition to the south side. We can't forget the lavatories either. The one we have now is so old that I'm constantly calling in a plumber to fix it! Besides, it would be nice to have two—one for the girls and one for the boys, instead of the single one we currently have."

There was muffled laughter all around. Mike Sanders stood. "Now, fellow council people, be fair. We can't just flush away our problems, can we? Equal lavatories for women and men— I'm all for it!"

Loud laughter followed this time. Mrs. Knightly tried to hush the group unsuccessfully.

"Please, everyone! I think we need to take Miss Turnbull seriously. She has asked for city funds to improve the library and we need to give her request the consideration it deserves. Let's take a vote..."

"I vote to table it so we can move onto more important items on the agenda. Besides, it's getting late. We all want to get home to our families, so I vote to discuss it at our next meeting," Rick Wood, the city manager, spoke.

"I second that!" Mike Sanders quickly added.

Candy Turnbull gathered her reports together and quickly left the room, thinking the council members were nothing more than a bunch of cretins. If she'd asked for money to fund a new baseball park, they'd have been falling all over themselves to help. She wished Mayor Simple was still alive. He, at least, knew the value of an updated library for the city.

Jay Lindt had remained silent throughout the entire meeting. He was thinking of his own troubles and couldn't be bothered with any insignificant ones the city might have. When he saw Kelli Sanderson waiting for him in the foyer, he hesitated for a moment, thinking how wrong he'd been to ever get involved with her, then ducked out through the back door before she could see him.

CHAPTER EIGHTEEN

"We'll be at the play tonight, me and the girls. I've got Zachy to babysit Wesley," Maggie's mom told her over dinner Friday night.

"Will you be in the play, mommy?" Susan asked.

"No, but I'll be playing the piano for it. If you listen carefully, you'll be able to hear me."

"Can we see you too?" Janie chimed in.

Maggie gave Wesley another spoonful of mashed potatoes. "No, I'll be behind the curtain, so you can't see me. But I'll find you afterwards."

A knock was heard coming from the backdoor then Zachy suddenly appeared inside the kitchen, ready to babysit. "I'm a bit early... sorry," he immediately apologized. "I could go home and wait for another half an hour if you want me to."

Maggie's mother put another plate on the table and told Zachy to sit down. "No, no...you're right on time. Would you like a piece of fried chicken? And help yourself to some potatoes and a roll."

Without hesitation, Zachy sat down and began to load his plate. Maggie and her mom exchanged smiles over the table, not surprised at all at Zach's early arrival, especially since fried chicken was involved.

"We put up our Christmas tree," Janie told him, 'in the parlor next to the piano. Do you have yours up yet?"

"No, my mom won't let us put it up until Christmas Eve," Zachy told them between mouthfuls of food.

"That's too bad," Janie sympathized. "Maybe if she saw ours, she'd let you put it up before that. Do you want to bring her over and let her see it? It has lights and bulbs and an angel at the top. It's really pretty."

Zachy smiled. "I'll go in the parlor and see it for myself when I'm through eating, how's that?"

Maggie got up from the table. "The chicken was delicious, Mom, as usual, but I'd better not eat too much before the play."

"You should at least have another roll before you leave."

"Thanks, Mom, but I'm good. I'll just start with the clean-up while you finish eating."

"I'll have the kids help me with the clean-up. You'll be late for the play if you don't get going. Isn't the orchestra supposed to be there early?"

"Yes, but nobody pays much attention to time—something about being a musician. Still, I guess I'd better be leaving soon."

"Then go and get ready. We can handle this, can't we, kids? And, take my car. I'll need yours to bring the girls," her mother shouted after her.

"I'll just walk," Maggie replied as she hurried up the stairs. "Then we can all ride home together when it's over."

Maggie bundled up in her warmest coat, boots, and scarf before leaving the house. Once outside, she was surprised to see it had started to snow again. She was also surprised to see Rob's jeep in the front of the house, parked and with the motor running.

"Thought you might like a ride," Rob hollered from his side window.

"Thanks, but I think I'd prefer walking tonight," Maggie answered. After overhearing the conversation he'd had with Brad Bennington, she had no desire to be involved any further with him or the case.

"Don't be silly—it's snowing! Besides, my jeep is nice and warm, and I really need to talk to you."

Maggie hesitated, then slowly crossed the lawn and reluctantly got into the jeep. "So, what do you want to talk to me about?"

"Getting right to the point, huh? No small talk to start things off?"

"It *is* a short ride to the old barn, you know. What's on your mind?"

Rob laughed. "Not much, to tell you the truth."

"Then, why did you say you needed to talk?"

Rob could see that Maggie was going to be difficult. For some reason or another, the inside of the jeep seemed to have gotten a bit chillier since her arrival, even though the heater was blowing out plenty of warm air.

"The cast party's tonight, over at the Summerhouse Inn. I was wondering if you'd like to go there with me—in my jeep."

"I kind of figured you'd take your jeep. The Summerhouse Inn *is* on the other side of town."

More iciness. Rob tried to think what he'd done to deserve this. "Well?" he asked.

"Thanks for the invite, but I wasn't planning on going. My mom and the girls are coming to see the play tonight and I want to spend the time with them afterwards. Sorry."

Rob pulled into a parking space close to the entrance of the barn. Maggie hopped out before he could say anything more, leaving him alone and completely at a loss as to what he had done wrong.

The play ran as smoothly as ever that night—the best performance yet—and everyone was in fine form. It had been running for two weeks with another two to go, and the cast and crew had all the glitches worked out by now. The small orchestra knew every cue by heart and no longer needed the promptings of Mrs. Barker, which was just as well, since she had other things on her mind tonight, what with the plans for the cast party afterwards.

"Maggie, the party is tonight," she'd told her at least a dozen times during the play. "You won't forget, will you?" Maggie smiled back, noncommittal.

When the play ended, Maggie left the theatre as quickly as she could before anyone else could ask her about the party. She made her way through the snow and ice outside, trying to find where her mom had parked the car when she had come with the girls. She finally found it behind the old barn. She got inside and turned the key in the ignition. *It would be nice to have it all warmed up,* she thought, when her mom and the girls came out.

When they arrived, they seemed to be talking all at once, telling Maggie how much they'd enjoyed the play. "It was fantastic!" her mother exclaimed. "And the music! I really liked it, especially the scene at Fezziwig's party!"

"We could hear you playing, mommy! Me and Susan were listening, like you told us," the girls said as they piled into the back seat. "It was the best play ever!"

"That's wonderful!" Maggie was content with her small, adoring fans.

"The woman who played the ghost of Christmas past was especially good—was she a professional actress? And, the guy who played Scrooge—Rob? Well, he was a hit with everyone! Isn't he the one who's been interested in you?" Maggie's mother was trying to be subtle.

"I think he would like to be, but it's not reciprocated. I'm not interested in him at all."

"Are you sure about that, dear?"

Maggie bristled a bit. She hated it when her mother saw through her.

When they got home, Wesley was asleep in his upstairs bedroom and Zachy was snoozing away on the sofa. Maggie took the girls upstairs to get them ready for bed while her mother woke Zachy to send him home. When Maggie came back downstairs, her mother was waiting for her at the foot of the stairs, looking confrontational.

"I overheard someone at the play say that the cast party was going to be at the Summerhouse Inn tonight," she said, accusingly. "You should have told me about it. We could've made it home all right without your help, you know. But, it's not too late to go. Hurry and get your coat back on. I'll watch the kids."

Maggie smiled at her mother, preparing for the argument that was to come. "I wasn't planning on going."

"And why not? Why have you been putting up with all the practicing and rehearsals for this play if you have no intention of taking advantage of the social side of it? Haven't I taught you anything? Besides, if you don't go, I'm sure you'll be missed by everyone, especially that nice man who plays Scrooge. It's obvious to me that he likes you, even if you can't see it. Wasn't he collaborating with you on this little mystery surrounding Dolores Simple's death? What happened with that?"

"I suppose we were collaborating, in a way," Maggie admitted, "but that was before this little mystery, as you call it, became a big one. Even you yourself told me not to fully trust him until we knew more about him."

"Yes, dear, but that was before I saw him in the play. He seems to be a very nice man, not at all the suspicious type."

"He's still part of it, though—the whole senseless thing," Maggie said, not wanting to get into the details of the conversation she'd overheard between Rob and Brad Bennington.

"And since Dolores's sister-in-law was killed—*murdered,* no less—I've decided it's time to leave the entire thing alone!"

"And that includes leaving Rob alone too? Really, Maggie!" Her mother seemed at the end of her wits. "Do you want to end up all alone, with nobody to love?"

"Now, that's not fair! I've got the girls and Wesley to love, and believe it or not, you too!"

Angry, Maggie turned and walked into the kitchen, ready for this discussion to be at an end. What she needed was a cool drink from the fridge. Her temper softened a bit when she saw the new displays of Wesley's artwork posted on the front of the refrigerator—crayon scribbles that had obviously been put there tonight with the help of Zachy and some fridge magnets.

She smiled as she looked at them, then slowly, her smile turned to horror.

"Mother!" she shouted as she took one of the pictures down. She ran to the front of the house.

"What? Maggie, what in the world...?"

Maggie held up the picture for her mother to see.

"You scared the living daylights out of me for this!? I don't see why Wesley's artwork is cause for concern. What's the matter with you?"

"Look at the paper he's drawn it on, not at the crayon marks! This paper is part of the minutes—those darn hospital minutes—that I handed over to Detective Milton! How did they get back here!?"

Maggie's mother looked closely at Wesley's paper. "Perhaps Detective Milton brought them back tonight when we were at the play," she suggested. "All I know is that there's got to be a perfectly good explanation for it—nothing to get all upset about, that's for sure."

"If Detective Milton brought them back, then where are the rest of the papers? Surely, he wouldn't just bring this one."

Maggie began looking frantically through the house, with her mother following closely behind.

First, into the kitchen, then the parlor, then quietly into the children's rooms upstairs. They continued to look in every corner of every room, until they finally found what they were looking for. There, at the very end of the upstairs hall, a trail of papers lay across the floor, just in front of Maggie's room.

Maggie picked one of them up, and then a second and a third. All of them were copies of the hospital minutes. When she opened her door, she saw more papers scattered everywhere around her room. Then she saw where they were coming from. The closet door was wide open, revealing the source of them all. It was a box—Hal's box from work—that she'd shoved unopened into the back of her closet when they'd moved in with Grandma. Apparently, Wesley had gotten into it tonight, scattering its contents all over her room and choosing a few to color on.

Maggie looked at each one closely. Some belonged to the folder marked *Hospital Board*, others were from random projects Hal had been working on before his death.

"What in the world..." her mother exclaimed.

"It's Hal's box," she told her. "All of these folders are from his work at the Trenton newspaper—things he'd been working on before he died. They represent a lot of unfinished articles, information that he thought was important enough to keep on file. And the hospital papers are here! They must be important after all, or Hal wouldn't have kept them!"

"Investigative reporting, yes." Maggie's mother was beginning to understand. "And tonight, his son Wesley decided to bring them all into the light by getting into something he shouldn't have."

"Like father, like son," Maggie whispered.

Maggie spread the papers out on the kitchen table, trying to get them in order as her mother sat quietly watching.

"This is new," she stated. "It's a list of the major contributors to the hospital building fund. Do you know any of these people?"

"Mary Simmington, Doris Davenport, Clyde Haswell, William Barlow and Frederick Rendell," Maggie's mom read off the list. "No, I can't say I do. However, the Davenports are a well-to-do family from Riverton. I wonder if this Doris was one of them."

"Look how much she donated! She must've been very well off if she could give away twenty-thousand dollars!"

"I wish I were half that lucky! All these people had to have been very rich. Look at the amounts they donated, and that was back in 1941! Some of them might not even be alive today, depending on how old they were when they first made these contributions. I wonder how we can find out. Shouldn't that be our first step, to find out if any of them are still alive?"

Maggie smiled. Apparently, they were back in, trying to unravel the mystery of the hospital minutes, but this time on behalf of her husband. She felt she owed it to him. After all, he'd gone to a lot of work, keeping his investigations on file, just like Dale Redding had said that first night the orchestra practiced. Dale had worked with Hal and knew how thorough he was at keeping records. He said that's what made Hal such a good reporter. *Well, maybe it's up to me to finish what he'd started,* Maggie thought—at least with this case. If she managed to finalize it, she would not only find closure for Hal but for herself as well. It was what she'd been missing all along, ever since Hal had left her so suddenly on that cold day last November.

"I'll take this list to Benson, at the playhouse," Maggie said. "Benson used to live in Trenton—Mrs. Barker told me—and he just might know some of these people. At least, it's worth a try."

"Benson, yes. He's that man who builds the sets. But, is he *that* old?"

"Mom, really? Have you ever seen him? He's definitely *that* old! I'll talk to him next week, at the performance."

"Yes. And you should get the other set of hospital minutes back from that detective you gave them to—to compare them with the ones we have here. Do you want me to call and make an appointment for you? I could call police headquarters and set something up."

"Really, mother! There's no need to bother them! I don't even want to get mixed up with the police—not with the murder they're currently investigating!"

"No, you're right. We don't need to bother the police— not yet. Want to join me in a cup of cocoa? It might help you sleep tonight. It's been a very long day and I know you have a lot on your mind—a lot to think about. What do you say?"

Maggie's mind was turning a mile a minute as she continued to look through Hal's file. "Sure, Mom. I think that just might be what we need right now."

CHAPTER NINETEEN

Detective Milton sat at his desk, waiting for the phone to ring. Almost a week had passed since Coralee Simples' suspicious death. The crime scene had been thoroughly gone over, yet nothing had been found, not even a nice incriminating fingerprint on the mahogany desk. Of course, Coralee's fingerprints were all over it, and Brad Bennington's too, for that matter. But that was not unusual. They had been the owners of the antique desk, after all.

The phone rang. As expected, it was Russ Secrist.

"Okay," Detective Milton said, "I'll meet you at the apartment. Yes, I remember." He hung up the phone and hurried out of his office. Russ Secrist had called to say he had found some new evidence, but Milton wasn't going to get his hopes up too high, not yet. Secrist was new at this, and what he thought was evidence might just be wishful thinking—something they'd all experienced before.

He opened the door at Number 17 and ducked under the police tape to enter. *This apartment*, he thought, *was much too modern-looking for his taste.* He liked the comfort of a worn-in, traditional décor.

"Is that you?" he heard Russ Secrist shout. "I'm over here, behind the desk."

Detective Milton followed the voice. "So, what do you have to show me?" he asked.

"Here, on the carpet—these small spots." Secrist was bending over, pointing at the spots.

Milton got down on his hands and knees to have a look. "There's three of them, the red marks right there. See?"

"They look like finger marks to me. Someone had to have had blood on their fingertips to make them. Have we tried lifting them for prints?"

"Yes, we tried, but no prints could be pulled."

Milton took a closer look. "They were probably made by Miss Simple herself. If she touched her head, then the carpet as she fell?"

"Yes, I'd thought of that. But there's one little problem. There wasn't any blood found on Miss Simple's fingertips."

Detective Milton stood to look at them from another angle. "So, you're suggesting that these were left by the murderer?"

"Since these same marks were found on Miss Simple's neck, then yes, I'm suggesting just that. The murderer probably got down like this, on his hands and knees, propping himself up with his left hand like this." Russ demonstrated as he explained. "Then, with the other hand, he felt Miss Simples' neck for a pulse, leaving behind identical marks with the other hand."

"Hmm… that sounds reasonable," Milton said. "But, without leaving any prints, it really doesn't do us much good, does it?"

"No, probably not."

"Too bad they couldn't pull any prints from them. The murderer was obviously wearing gloves."

"Yes, but, most gloves—the kind we wear in the winter to keep our hands warm—would've smeared the blood. These spots are nice and neat—not made by any fabric I can think of."

"Leather gloves could've made them." Milton held up his own leather gloves to show him. "See how smooth the fingertips are?"

"Yeah, I guess they could've made the marks. But, as snug as leather fits on your fingers, it still wouldn't make these tidy little stains. What about cleaning gloves? You know, the kind ladies wear when they're working around the house? They're tight-fitting enough to make these marks. Perhaps we need to look in that direction. Did Coralee Simple have a maid—perhaps the same one Dolores Simple had?"

"If you mean Maggie Brown— well, she wasn't really Dolores's maid. Remember, she told us when we went to talk to her. Just a friend, helping out."

"But perhaps she was posing as one, like before. Anyway, I doubt that Coralee Simple was one to do her own cleaning."

"No, she's not the type to do her own housework. Why don't you check and see if she has one—someone regular, before we go looking at Maggie Brown again. By the way, have you had time to look over Brad Bennington's alibi?"

"You mean the one where he said he was at his office working?"

"Is there another one?"

"His secretary confirmed he was in the office at the time Miss Simple was murdered, but the doorman downstairs said he'd been out all day."

"So, his involvement in the crime is still undetermined?"

"Apparently."

Detective Milton looked at his watch. "I need to get back to the office. I have a ton of paperwork to finish. Do you have anything else to show me?"

"Just this." Russ Secrist handed Milton a ticket. It was green, about one inch by two. "We found this on the floor, behind the curtain over there—close to where the body was found."

Detective Milton looked it over, then reached in his pocket for his glasses. "Can't see a thing without these," he said. "What does it say?"

"It's a ticket for *A Christmas Carol*. Apparently, it's a play they're putting on over in Springville at the theatre in the old barn."

"Really? What's the date on it?"

"December 19th. It's on a Saturday, at seven o'clock. Seat Number 23A"

Detective Milton put the ticket into an evidence bag and gave it back to Russ Secrist. "Check it for fingerprints," he told him. "And keep this date open. We might just have to make time to visit Mrs. Trudy Barker—she's the director there, at the old barn. Puts on a mighty fine play too. Have you ever been to one of them?"

"Can't say as I have," Russ answered flatly. "I'm really not a fan of the theatre."

"Well, keep the date open, just in case we need to go. We can have a night out, just the two of us, at the old Springville barn. How does that sound?"

"Oh, goodie," was all Russ Secrist could manage to say.

"And get a sample of those blood stains for the lab to look at. They might have something to tell us after all."

Malcolm Graves had been watching Coralee's apartment since eight o'clock that morning. He was parked half a block away in order not to attract any attention to himself. The police had been in and out of the building all morning and into the late afternoon too, looking for clues in the high-rise apartment. Even when night fell, and the lights from Coralee's third story window shone out from above, did he continue to wait, immovable. Finally, when he saw the lights go out and the last two detectives leave the building and drive away, did he dare step out of his nondescript Ford Escort to stretch his tired legs.

He let himself into the apartment with the key Coralee had given him months ago when all was still right with them. He scoffed at himself, knowing he should have known better. Coralee, after all, only cared about herself and never about anyone else. She'd had two husbands before him, after all. Why would he think he could make her change? He decided it was best to put her out of his mind to concentrate on what he'd come for. Good thing he knew about the desk's hidden drawer. Coralee would have been livid had she known her brother had shown him the secret compartment sometime after they'd married.

Using a small flashlight, he made his way over to the desk and opened the secret compartment without any difficulty. He quickly found the papers and transferred them to his briefcase.

Then silently, he made his way out of the apartment and closed the door behind him. *There was a certain finality to the act of closing the door,* he thought. This chapter in his life was over and he was glad to be moving away from it.

CHAPTER TWENTY

Mrs. Fran Knightly had two agendas in mind as she entered the mayor's office the next morning. One, she needed to find some information on Mayor Simple for the newspaper article she'd been assigned to write in his memory. Second, she was keen on finding anything she could about the hospital board. She didn't get her hopes up too high on the latter though—too many years had gone by—but she nevertheless felt an obligation towards Maggie Brown to at least try.

The best part about snooping around Mayor Simple's office was that, as mayor pro-temp, *I have every right to,* she thought smugly. Besides, who else was going to clean out the office and get it ready for the next mayor who was to be appointed in the new year.

She sat down at the desk and began opening drawers and pulling out folders to read. Signed copies of the contract with Industry-Man—the newest development on the north end of town—were there, along with plans for a new road to get their employees out to the plant. She frowned.

If Industry-Man Enterprises was hoping to get the city of Trenton to pay for that road, they had another think coming. She wondered if Mayor Simple had had plans of moving this through the city council. *It would've been just like him to,* she thought. He never could turn anyone down.

She pulled out more files, mostly just records of city ordinances, then put them back again, disappointed. What she needed was some personal information on the mayor—something that would sound nice in an article. The only thing personal she could find so far was the picture of his wife Dolores that sat on the corner of his desk and the blue windbreaker that hung on the back of his door.

She moved over to the file cabinet and began reading the labels on each folder there. Again, nothing personal, only city related. At the very back of the bottom drawer, and much to her surprise, she found a folder marked *Hospital Minutes—1941. How wonderfully unexpected*, she thought. Now she really could call Maggie Brown and tell her she'd found something after all!

She pulled out the folder and opened it, only to find it was empty. Why, she wondered, would the mayor have an empty folder on file? Surely, the papers must be around somewhere, waiting to be put back in their place. She left the mayor's office and headed down the hall towards Dick Wood's office. Perhaps he'd know something about it.

"This isn't the first time I've heard about those hospital papers," Dick said, leaning back in his chair.

"Of course, it isn't. I left you a message, weeks ago, to see if you could track them down. Maggie Brown—do you remember her? She was asking about them for a friend and I told her I'd find out what I could."

"Well, a detective named Milton was here too, just yesterday, asking me what I knew about them. I can't, for the life of me, see why they'd be of any interest to anyone. Do you know how old they are? And you say Maggie Brown asked you about them as well? My, my…" He stopped to rub his chin. "Maybe it's time for me to dig deep and see what I can find. For being so old—not to mention missing from their folder—they seem to be making the rounds!"

"Why was Detective Milton looking for them? Did he say?"

"No. But you know detectives. They keep things pretty close to the vest, not wanting to cause any unnecessary gossip or concern, until they can unravel whatever mystery they're involved with. They just like to ask a lot of questions—they never want to answer any."

"Hmmm…makes you wonder though. Perhaps I should have another visit with Maggie Brown. Perhaps she's not telling everything she knows."

Maggie had systematically been going through phone books trying to find the names of the hospital contributors she'd found among Hal's papers. When that proved a dead end, she'd decided it was time to talk to Benson.

She found him in the old barn the next morning, fixing one of the sets that had come loose on its hinge. When she showed him the list, he put down his flat-head screwdriver and adjusted the glasses on his face.

"Dead. Dead. Dead and buried…Dead," he announced as he silently read down the list. "No, wait a minute here. This one, Clyde Haswell, is in a nursing home over in Clarksdale—or, at least, that's what I heard."

"Does he have any relatives who are local?" Maggie wasn't sure she wanted to make the two-hour drive to Clarksdale.

Benson laughed uncharacteristically. "No, not him. No family at all, to speak of. He never got married. Too busy chasing the all-mighty dollar, he was!"

"Not like you. I've heard you have quite the family. Seven children!"

"Add eighteen grandchildren to the mix and yer about right. Oh, and three great-grandchildren."

"That's wonderful! There's nothing like family to complete your happiness." Maggie smiled at him. Who would have thought that this man, who seemed to be quite the loner, actually had so many people in his life.

"Yes, good ol' families—there's nothing like them to make yer life a misery, if yer not careful!" Now it was his turn to smile. Maggie nodded understandingly and thanked him for his help.

When she got back home, her mother was anxiously waiting to hear what she had to say.

Maggie told her about Clyde Haswell.

"Really? That's good to hear! So, one of the contributors is, actually still alive and living in a nursing home over in Clarksdale!"

"Yes, and I think I need to make a visit to him when things slow down a bit here."

"Maggie, you know you'll be waiting a long time for that to happen! Why don't you just go now? I know you don't have any piano lessons today, and I can watch the kids—we can finish our Christmas baking. They can help me decorate the cookies we made. Besides, you need a day off by yourself.

Maybe you can get in some Christmas shopping too, while you're out. Make a whole day of it!"

The thought of having a whole day to herself was appealing. Maggie hugged her mother.

"What would I do without you?"

"Lots of time to find that out, but today's not the day! Just go while the day is still young, and before I change my mind!"

Maggie grabbed her purse and coat and headed out the door, ready to do some serious investigating on her own.

CHAPTER TWENTY-ONE

"Mr. Haswell, you have a visitor. Are you through with your breakfast tray?"

The nurse led Maggie into a small, well-furnished room.

"Take it. And don't bring me toast again. I asked for a bagel, not toast"! The old man sat in an over-stuffed chair by his bed, a tray of food in front of him. He was small and shriveled but seemed to have enough gruffness going for him to make up for the frail state he appeared to be in.

The nurse took away the tray. "He's all yours," she said to Maggie as she walked out the door.

"I don't know why they can't get it right," Mr. Haswell continued to grumble. "A bagel doesn't look anything like a burnt piece of old bread. Everyone knows the difference between bagels and toast." He looked directly at Maggie. "Do you know the difference between bagels and toast?"

Maggie wasn't sure how to answer such a question. She decided to turn the conversation around and begin asking some questions of her own.

"Mr. Haswell, I'm Maggie Brown. I understand that you donated some money to a hospital fund, back in 1941. Do you remember donating to that?"

Mr. Haswell brightened up momentarily. "You must be here about the plaque that's supposed to be put up in the hospital foyer! You know, they haven't gotten around to doing it yet, even after all these years. What in the world is wrong with people? You can't trust anybody to do what they say they would!"

Maggie was confused. "So, you are the Mr. Haswell who made the contribution to the hospital in Trenton?"

"Haven't you been listening! Of course, I am! And they told me there'd be a plaque with my name inscribed on it and that it would be displayed there, in the foyer, for everyone to see!"

"What plaque is that, Mr. Haswell? Maggie asked, a bit frustrated.

"The one at the hospital! Last time I was there, I went to see that young Doctor White about my heart, you know—it hasn't been working very well since I had that stroke back in '79. Well, I was supposed to go there and have some tests the doctor had ordered, and while I was there, I had the nurse walk me through the foyer from one end to the other. Well, I couldn't find it anywhere! So, I told her to take me to the front desk so I could ask those ladies about it. Darned if they didn't know anything either, the silly old things! So, I asked Doctor White —after the tests were over, you see—I asked him, *do you know where they put the plaque—the one with my name on it?* And do you think he even listened to what I said? As much as I pay him, you'd think he'd listen to me?! Imbeciles! I never should've given them my money!"

"Let me get this straight. Someone promised you they would put up a plaque in the foyer of the hospital to honor you as a contributor?"

"Yes! Isn't that what I've been saying? All of us who donated were told we'd have our names displayed in the foyer —on a plaque! Well, they haven't done it yet, and after all these years, they probably won't do it at all, the darn weasels!"

"I'm so sorry, Mr. Haswell. But, why didn't you complain about it back then?"

"Humph! I moved to Florida in '42. I didn't know they hadn't put it up until I got back. All this time, I supposed there would be a plaque!"

Maggie was starting to see the whole picture now. "Mr. Haswell— let me check into this for you. Apparently, something has gone very wrong."

"You're telling me!"

"I'll check into it and let you know what I find. Don't worry; we'll get to the bottom of this, one way or another."

Mr. Haswell calmed down a bit. "Good," he said, "and, when you leave, will you go 'round to the kitchen and tell them I don't want toast anymore? Really, am I to be constantly surrounded by imbeciles who can't tell a bagel from a piece of toast?!"

Maggie slipped out of the room, unnoticed. Mr. Haswell was too preoccupied with his ranting to notice she'd left. She drove for an hour, thinking about what he'd told her. By the time she got to the Trenton exit, she'd made up her mind. She was going to stop at the hospital and look for herself. Perhaps Mr. Haswell had missed it before, or perhaps it was in another place.

If such a plaque existed, she was confident that she would be able to find it.

She parked in the visitor's area, then entered through the large front doors that led to the lobby. She shuddered, remembering the last time she'd been there and started having second thoughts about coming. Quickly, Maggie's eyes scanned the many plaques that were displayed on the walls of the foyer. There were a lot of them—many people and organizations had been given recognition for their humanitarian services in the form of an engraved plaque— but nothing with Mr. Haswell's name on it could be found, or any of the other contributors from Hal's list. For the next forty minutes or so, she walked up and down the hallways of the hospital, looking for the specific plaque and not finding it.

Discouraged, Maggie walked back to the lobby. The clock on the wall showed it was later than she'd thought. She took one last look at the plaques that hung there, then headed for the exit. In her hurry to leave, she bumped into a lady who was also trying to exit. "Excuse me," she said, a bit embarrassed.

"Maggie?" the woman asked. "Yes, it is you! Maggie Brown, how are you? You're not here because… well, is one of your children sick? Or have you been in an accident?" She looked Maggie over with concern.

Maggie gave the woman standing in front of her a big hug. "Mrs. Bolger!" she exclaimed.

"How nice to see you. No, nobody's sick or anything."

"That's good to hear!"

"So, you're still working here as a pink lady… that's nice."

"Well, yes. I should retire—Roy wants me to. But they really need volunteer help and I can't very well leave them high and dry now, can I?"

"No, you can't!" Maggie smiled at her former neighbor, remembering how she was always ready to help everyone she could. "But, you're just on your way home now, aren't you? As much as I'd love to have some time to visit with you, I know you must be on your way."

"Nonsense," Mrs. Bolger replied as she sat down on one of the benches against the lobby wall. "Sit down and tell me how you've been! And, your children...tell me all about them."

Maggie sat down beside her and answered the many questions she had then asked some of her own.

"We've got new neighbors in your house, you know," Mrs. Bolger said in answer to one of Maggie's questions. "They're new to Trenton—well, new six months ago. He works at Industry Man and she stays at home, raising her four children. They're good neighbors, but not like you and Hal were. You were more like family than neighbors."

Maggie was touched with her words. "And you were like family too," she replied. "We loved living next door to you and Roy."

"What brings you here today? Are you visiting someone in the hospital? Trenton is a little out of your way, isn't it?"

"I've just been over to Clarksdale, visiting a Mr. Clyde Haswell in the nursing home there and decided to stop here on my way home to check on something for him. Do you know him? He lived in Trenton—oh, a while back."

"The name doesn't sound familiar. Are you related to him?"

"No, my husband Hal was doing an article on him before he died. I'm just checking up on him. He claims that he donated money to this hospital in the early days and that they promised to put up a plaque to honor him, here in the foyer."

"And, you've come to see if it's here?"

"Yes. But I haven't found anything with his name on it."

"You know, that reminds me of something similar. Roy was reading the obituaries in the newspaper, oh, it's been a while back. He always reads them to see if anyone he knows has died, and he came across one that said the same thing—about some money that was donated to the hospital to get it started. You know how the loved one's families like to brag on about the accomplishments of their dearly departed in the obituaries? Well, this woman—I believe it was a woman—she'd supposedly donated a lot of money too, to the hospital—kind of like your Mr. Haswell has claimed to have done."

"How long ago was that?" Maggie was suddenly interested.

"I believe it was last year, in the spring. I remember it was in the spring because I'd just brought in some lilacs from our bushes. You know, the ones from the west side of the house? Well, I was putting them in a vase when Roy told me about it."

"Do you remember the woman's name?" Maggie asked.

"Oh, no, dear. I'm doing well to remember the obituary."

"Could it have been Mary Simmington?" Maggie tried to jog her memory. "Or Doris Davenport?"

"Doris Davenport! Yes, that's right!" Mrs. Bolger seemed pleased with herself. "I remember it was one of the Davenports from Riverton because Roy said he knew the family! But how did you know it was her?"

"They were on Hal's list also," Maggie briefly stated.

"Oh, I see." Mrs. Bolger really didn't see the connection but didn't care. She was just happy to have helped Maggie out.

"Well, although it's been nice catching up with you, I'd better not detain you any further. What would Roy think, you coming home late for dinner?" Maggie stood to leave. "He'd probably think the worst—that I'd been in an accident or something!" She laughed. "Even if I was, I'm at the right place to get treated for it!"

Suddenly, Mrs. Bolger became very serious. She put a hand on Maggie's shoulder and looked at her with concern.

"You know, the night of Hal's accident, the hospital staff was stretched pretty thin," she explained. "A lot of the nurses— and doctors too— couldn't get here because of the storm, so many of the roads had been closed that night. The staff who'd just completed a long shift couldn't leave until they were replaced, so they had no option but to keep on working. And, the accidents! The emergency room was overflowing!" She turned away from Maggie briefly to wipe away a tear. "And, your Hal," she said, her voice faltering. "I'm so sorry about Hal... so sorry. But, on the bright side, I'm glad you were able to have that sweet baby of yours without any complications. Thank goodness for tender mercies that do come our way!"

Yes, thank goodness for them, Maggie thought. She gave Mrs. Bolger one last hug then walked out with her through the lobby doors.

CHAPTER TWENTY-TWO

The presents under the tree were getting higher and higher each day in the cozy little parlor at Grandma's house. The brightly wrapped boxes, in festive red and green colored paper and large bows, were pouring out from under the boughs of the tree, promising an abundant Christmas.

Today, they were being admired by Susan who was sitting in the loft above, her bare feet dangling between the railings.

"It's so pretty, Mama," she said in her tiny voice when Maggie asked her what she was doing up there. "I just like to look down at it."

Maggie climbed the stairs and sat on the floor beside her. "You're right, Susan! It's very pretty from up here!"

It wasn't long before Janie and Wesley had come out of their rooms to join them. he four of them sat perched above the parlor, like birds on a post. When Grandma came through the front door, back from another shopping trip, and added more gifts to the pile, she pretended not to see them.

"I wonder where everyone is," she said in a loud voice, smiling.

Janie and Susan started to giggle, giving away their hiding place. "We're here, Grandma!"

"Who's up there spying on me? You're like a bunch of Santa's elves, trying to catch someone being bad."

"Or good," Susan added.

"Who's ready for a snack?" Grandma asked. "I bought doughnuts!"

Janie and Susan ran down the hall towards the back stairs, trying to beat Grandma to the kitchen. Maggie picked up Wesley, ready to follow them, when she heard the doorbell ring. She quickly unlatched the safety gate at the top of the stairs and hurried down to answer it, with Wesley perched on her hip.

"Delivery for Maggie Brown," a young man said from behind a bunch of red roses.

"I'm Maggie Brown."

"Then sign here, please." He handed her a clipboard.

Quickly, Maggie signed it and took the flowers inside. Immediately, she looked for a card and found a small one tucked inside the bouquet.

The words *Meet me after the play tonight?* were written across the elegantly embossed card.

It was signed *Rob.*

"I really don't need this right now," Maggie said out loud, suddenly irritated with the beautiful roses. Before she could stop him, Wesley had grabbed a handful of the red petals in his chubby fingers and was trying to put them in his mouth. She immediately pried them out of his hands.

"And *you* don't need this either!" she said, scolding him for trying to eat the petals.

"Who are the flowers from?" her mom asked as Maggie walked into the kitchen carrying the bouquet in one arm and balancing Wesley in the other.

"Rob Stanger."

"Why, they're beautiful! And fragrant too! Here, let me find you a vase."

Maggie's mother found the perfect vase under the sink and filled it with water. Soon, the arrangement was sitting in the middle of the kitchen table for everyone to enjoy.

"Anything you want to tell me?" her mother asked, grinning at her daughter.

"Not really. Apparently, Rob wants to see me after the play tonight."

"Ohhh…???"

Maggie broke off a piece of her doughnut and handed it to Wesley, who'd already eaten a bite of Susan's and had powdered sugar all over his face.

"Look at Wesley!" Janie was giggling. "He looks like Santa Claus with a white beard!"

Susan started to giggle too. "Mommy, look! Hurry, before he licks it off!"

Maggie smiled. "Maybe he *is* the real Santa Claus! Who knows?"

"So, are you going to meet with him?" Maggie's mother persisted.

"I don't know," Maggie answered, half irritated. "It's not really that big of a deal whether I see him or not. He was only interested in me, in the first place, because of the papers he thought I had."

"Really, Maggie. Why would he send you flowers if he wasn't interested in you? But, if you're not interested back, well, then that's another matter altogether."

Maggie went to the sink to get a wet rag to clean Wesley with. She was ready to end this conversation. She took the roses off the table and moved them to the counter by the sink, determined to forget all about them. Out of sight, out of mind.

That night at the playhouse, she discovered another long-stemmed rose—a single red blossom lying across her music stand. It had obviously been put there to remind her of Rob's request to meet him after the play. She quickly moved it to the top of the piano, wondering why Rob had to complicate things like this. Tomorrow was the last performance, and after that, there would be no reason to see him again. She had to admit that she'd miss his company but, even then, she couldn't quite forget how he'd acted when she'd shown him the hospital papers and then later, when he was talking in his office with Brad Bennington. Was he mixed up with Coralee's murder? It was something she couldn't quite get past.

The play seemed to drag on tonight, at least for Maggie. The old barn was full to capacity and the audience was great, but Maggie was in a mood. She wanted the play to end soon and the night to be over. She dreaded seeing Rob afterwards and started to devise a way to leave as soon as it was over to avoid talking to him altogether. Perhaps she'd talk to him later, when she had things figured out.

"Look at that audience! Can you believe it?" Mrs. Barker was peering out of the curtain just before intermission, excited at the large turnout. "And tomorrow night will be even better! The last performance is always the best! First timers, along with second and third timers—those who loved the play so much they want to see it again—will be here tomorrow, you'll see!" She did a little skip as she closed the curtain to lead the music for the entre'acte.

What seemed like an eternity to Maggie but was only an hour later, she found herself racing through the exit music, once again, ready to end the play. She'd put her coat on before the music started so she'd be ready to make a quick escape. She knew Rob would be too busy doing curtain calls, along with the other actors and actresses on stage, to notice her retreat.

Just as she was about to leave the orchestra pit, Dale Redding stopped her.

"Hey, Maggie! Do you have a minute?" he asked as she passed by his drums.

"Well… maybe a minute." Maggie was reluctant but didn't want to appear rude.

"Here, let me put these away first." Dale proceeded to put his drumsticks inside their plastic cover while Maggie stood nervously by, watching him fumble then drop them. One of them rolled under a chair.

"Ahh, Dale… I'm in a bit of a hurry. Could it wait until tomorrow?"

"Oh, sorry. If I thought it could wait, I wouldn't think of keeping you from leaving." He paused to retrieve the run-away drumstick. "Now, what is it that I'm keeping you from?"

Maggie sighed. "It's just that I need to go, you know—the kids and all. I really need to be getting home."

Dale smiled at her. "Maggie, really. If I know your mom, she'll have gotten them to bed long ago."

Maggie sat down on the chair that was recently left vacant by the trombonist. "Okay, Dale. What's so important?"

Dale paused, as if trying to find the right words. "It's the key change in the entre'acte, there on measure forty-eight, page four." He slowly turned to the spot in his music. By now, they were the only two left in the orchestra pit.

"What about it, Dale? As a drummer, I don't see how a key change applies to you."

"You're right…it doesn't. Except for—well, can you turn to it in your music and I'll show you?"

Impatiently, Maggie opened her music and found the measure. "Here it is. Now, what's the problem?"

Dale leaned over to have a look. "No, no. That's not the right place," he said, taking Maggie's music and flipping through it, trying to find the trouble spot.

Maggie suddenly stood, her hands on her hips. "Dale, really! What are you trying to do? I've really got to go now, so whatever reason you have for stalling me will have to wait until…"

"Ah, here's the reason now."

Maggie turned to see Rob Stanger walk through the curtains and into the orchestra pit. He still had on his costume and makeup.

"Thanks, Dale. I'll take it from here," he said.

Dale gathered his music and started to leave. "Sorry, Maggie," he said, smiling knowingly. "Nothing personal, you understand."

Maggie sat back down in the vacant chair, feeling defeated.

"So, you got Dale to detain me? Really, Rob?"

Rob smiled at her. "Dale's a good man. Besides, I knew you'd try to duck out before I had a chance to talk to you and I —well, I really need you to explain something to me— something I'm having a hard time understanding."

"What do you need to understand?' Maggie said, trying to be patient.

Rob sat down beside her. "I need to understand why you've been avoiding me lately."

Maggie looked down at her lap, not sure how to put it. "Brad Bennington…" she started to say. She wanted to explain that she knew he was working for him.

"What about him?" Rob interrupted. "He hasn't asked you out, has he?"

Maggie briefly thought of the incident with Brad on the cellar stairs. She smiled. "As a matter of fact, he did!"

"I see. So, that's why you've been avoiding me?"

"No, it isn't! Besides, Brad rescinded his offer as soon as he found out about my kids."

"Yeah, that sounds like Brad—the idiot."

"If he's an idiot, then why are you working for him?" Maggie blurted out.

"Ah… so that's it." Rob slowly shook his head. "You don't like Brad, so you don't like that I'm working for him. Well, I'm not working for him—not anymore. How did *you* know I'd been working for him?"

Maggie looked a bit guilty. "Never mind how I knew."

"So, you've been avoiding me because I was working for Brad Bennington? That doesn't make a whole lot of sense, Maggie. You know I work as a private investigator. Why shouldn't I have him for a client?"

"There's no reason at all that you shouldn't," Maggie said, genuinely sorry she'd brought it up in the first place. It was much too complicated to explain. "By the way, thank you for the roses," she said, trying to change the subject.

Rob looked at her, encouraged for the first time tonight. "I was hoping you'd like them."

"Of course, I did. What's not to like?"

"Then, how about going out with me sometime?"

Maggie was speechless. "Haven't you heard?" she tried for a bit of humor, "I've got three kids! Are you sure you want to?"

"Yes, I heard a rumor along those lines. But there's absolutely no problem there. Unlike some people I know, I like kids! And since tomorrow's our last performance, I thought you might like to go to dinner with me afterwards—sort of a celebration. You can even bring those kids of yours, if you want!"

Maggie faltered, trying to come up with just the right words. "Rob... I can't," she finally said. "I don't know why. I like you and all. I just can't get past..." Her voice trailed off, not sure how to finish her sentence.

Rob stood to go. He took off his top hat and looked Maggie squarely in the eyes. "Try to get past it soon, Maggie." His voice was soft and calm, genuinely making her feel even worse than before. "Believe it or not, I do know how you feel. But, for your own good, try to get past it as soon as you can."

Then he opened the curtain and disappeared down the hall and into the dressing room. Maggie waited a few minutes before trying to leave. She was feeling all mixed up inside and was wishing hard that she wasn't.

CHAPTER TWENTY-THREE

It was the last night of the play. Detective Milton and Russ Secrist had just arrived at the old barn.

"It looks like a full house—are you sure we need to go in? I don't think there's going to be any room for us," Russ Secrist announced, not too happy about having to sit through a boring play tonight. There had to be a better way to find the person who'd left the ticket at the murder scene.

"Yes, we need to go in," Detective Milton spoke decisively. "I called ahead to reserve us some seats, so you don't have to worry if there's going to be room for us. Besides, you're going to enjoy yourself, trust me! Trudy Barker always puts on an entertaining play."

"I thought we were supposed to be working on the investigation. Are you sure it's okay to enjoy ourselves when we're supposed to be hard at work? It doesn't seem right to me somehow."

"Stop grumbling. Haven't you ever heard of the saying 'all work and no play'?"

"No, I haven't. But I'm okay with the no play part. I don't particularly like them."

Detective Milton gave up, exasperated. He was determined to enjoy a night out at the theatre, even if he had to drag his grumpy junior partner along. Entering the lobby, he immediately surveyed his surroundings. There were a lot of people there, just like Russ had said, and all contained in one old barn. His job was to separate them into suspects— individuals who may or may not have committed a murder. One thing he knew for sure, there was an excellent chance that the real murderer was here tonight. He smiled, thoroughly enjoying himself.

Suddenly, Russ Secrist's pager went off. He ducked outside to use the car radio to call dispatch, hoping against hope that he'd be needed elsewhere tonight. When he got back inside, he quickly found Milton who was getting a huge tub of popcorn at the concession stand.

He pulled him aside and explained what he'd just heard.

"I guess it's your lucky day, Secrist," Detective Milton told him. "Take the police car and head for the airport. Maybe you can get there in time to intercept the alleged suspect. I'll stay here and work things on this end."

Without further delay and before Detective Milton could change his mind, Russ Secrist hurried out of the theatre, smiling at the fortunate turn of events in his favor.

In the lobby, Selma and her husband were also standing in line to buy some popcorn. They had come to the play with Mary Addison and her husband, Pastor Addison. The Addisons had just purchased a new house with the help of Selma's Real Estate Office and were excited to be their guests tonight at the play.

"This playhouse is quite impressive," Mary was telling Selma, "or, should I say, 'play-barn'?" Selma laughed appropriately at Mary's attempt at humor, even though she didn't think it was funny in the least. "Wait until you see the play. That's what's *really* impressive, isn't it, Si?" Selma turned to her husband briefly then continued talking through his answer. "You know when you come to Springville for a play that you won't be disappointed in the least! It makes you wonder why Trenton doesn't have a playhouse of its own!"

"Where would they find the actors to be in it?" Si asked doubtfully, finally getting a word in.

"Oh, I'm sure people would step up and do their part, if given the opportunity. I know *I* would!"

"And, speaking of people from Trenton, look who's just arrived, over there by the front entrance. It's Kelli Sanderson!"

Selma glanced over in the direction Mary had indicated. "I don't see her with anyone. I wonder if she came alone."

Selma and Mary followed their husbands as they carried the drinks and popcorn into the theatre.

"You know, I saw her the other day with Jay Lindt from the city offices. I wonder if Kelli and Jay are seeing each other," Selma commented as she and Mary climbed the risers to their seats.

"Perhaps he'll be coming tonight too. Look, she just sat down there, on the other side of the theatre. We can keep watch," said Selma.

"Keep watch? What are you talking about?" her husband asked, confused.

Selma turned to Mary, ignoring him. "Yes, we have a good view. We can easily see if someone joins up with her later. Wouldn't it be a kicker if it *did* turn out to be Jay?"

Behind the scenes, and between the dressing rooms and the orchestra pit, Mrs. Barker was hurrying back and forth, frantically making sure everything and everybody was in place and ready to go. Just as she'd predicted the night before, the playhouse was full. She even had to ask Benson to set up some folding chairs in the back on the ramp for the expected overflow. *Maybe we could squeeze in a few in the front too,* she thought, to accommodate any latecomers.

Maggie Brown had just arrived and was trying to make her way through the crowded lobby. She was a bit later than usual, she knew, and hoped Mrs. Barker wasn't fretting over it. By the look of it, Mrs. Barker probably had a million other things to deal with and wasn't noticing the missing pianist, at least not yet.

As she passed by the tall Christmas tree in the lobby, Maggie was stopped by Fran Knightly. She was wearing an outdated but expensive looking coat, complete with a fur collar.

"Maggie! How nice to see you here, at the playhouse!"

"It's nice to see you too. Is anyone with you?"

"No, I came alone tonight. I do a lot of things alone—ever since my husband passed away. Are you here by yourself as well?" Mrs. Knightly seemed hopeful. "We could sit together if you are. I'm sure we could arrange it—exchange seats with someone—if you wanted to."

Maggie smiled, feeling a bit sorry for her. "Thanks, but I'll be sitting on the piano bench all evening, there behind the curtain."

"Oh, of course! You're the accompanist! You know, this play has been advertised all over Trenton," she explained. "Everywhere you go, there are flyers telling you to go to the old Springville barn and see the Christmas play. I even saw our librarian, Candy Turnbull, over by the concessions. She must've seen the flyers too!"

"Yes, we seem to have a great turnout tonight. Mrs. Barker sees to that. And, speaking of Mrs. Barker, I'd better get to the orchestra pit now. I don't want her to think I'm not coming! Perhaps I'll see you afterwards?"

"Yes, as a matter of fact, I do need to talk to you about something important—something I found, or rather, didn't find."

Maggie was intrigued but didn't have time to ask Mrs. Knightly what she was talking about.

"How about we meet during intermission?" she suggested. "We could talk then. You could meet me behind the curtain by the piano, there in the orchestra pit."

"Perfect. I'll see you then!"

The lights in the theatre started to dim as people hurried to their seats. Suddenly, the orchestra began the overture. Maggie hurried to the pit and quickly got into place. She opened her music and began to play, noticing the look Mrs. Barker gave her. *Oh well, there isn't anything I can do about it now,* she thought. Soon, the lights were dimmed in the theatre and the voice of the narrator giving the opening lines was heard once again. Then the lights came back on and Scrooge's cold, dank office from an era long ago miraculously appeared on the stage.

Marley was dead, to begin with. There is no doubt whatever about that. The register of his burial was signed by the clergyman, the undertaker, and the chief mourner. Scrooge signed it.

And Scrooge's name was good upon 'Change for anything he chose to put his hand to.' Old Marley was as dead as a doornail...

Mrs. Barker was in her usual place, peeking out of the curtain from inside the orchestra pit, excited at the turnout. The extra chairs Benson had set up were filled as well as all the others in the theatre. She glanced across the audience. Wait, there was one seat in the A section that was still empty! She looked closer, noticing there was a coat lying across its back. She realized someone must be saving it. *Okay—that one would be filled later,* she thought, but she was going to keep an eye on it all the same.

Maggie noticed that the other musicians in the pit seemed to be taking even more liberties tonight than they usually did. Snacks were generously being passed around, for one thing. Dale had brought two dozen doughnuts to share and Melissa and Karen, the flutists, had brought a big bag of Tootsie Rolls and licorice. Mrs. Wilson, the clarinetist, had brought two tubs of popcorn from the concession stand to add to the impromptu buffet, making Mrs. Barker run for napkins when buttery fingers became too slippery to play instruments. *Closing night, at least here in the orchestra pit, seemed to be party time*, Maggie thought, surprised that Mrs. Barker allowed it.

The play moved forward, well received by the audience's enthusiastic applause. In due course, each scene was acted out and each song was sung in its proper place. It wasn't long before the stage crew, in their black attire, were setting up the props for the final scene of act one, just before intermission.

The scene had Scrooge entering on stage right, with the ghost of Christmas Past who was played by Melanie Cook. She was dressed in a long silk gown and held a wand in her hand.

The stage now had recreated the counting house of young Scrooge who was sitting behind his desk, carefully tallying the marks in his ledger. From stage left, his fiancé entered, cool and stately in her blue Victorian dress, with a look of resolve on her heavily powdered face. With lots of dramatic effect, she gave the young Scrooge back his ring and told him he was now free of his obligation to her. Scrooge, surprised, asked if he'd ever shown reason to want to be released.

You fear the world too much, she answered gently yet firmly. '*All your other hopes have merged into the hope of being beyond the chance of its sordid reproach...*'

Maggie squirmed a bit. This part always made her feel a bit uncomfortable. Did she fear the world too much as well? She hadn't when Hal was beside her. She felt like she could conquer anything with him by her side. But now he was gone, and things were different—*she* was different.

The violins, cued unnecessarily by Mrs. Barker, started the sad background music for the scene. Maggie came in next on the piano. The music continued softly until the end when old Scrooge asked the ghost of Christmas Past to remove him from the unbearable memory. Then the lights on stage dimmed slowly until the stage was left in total darkness. After a sensational pause, the lights in the audience came back on and the illusion of the theatre was replaced, once again, by reality. It was time for intermission.

Mrs. Barker immediately peeked out of the curtain again. "Drats!" she exclaimed. "That seat is still empty—the one with the coat draped over it! Here we're turning people away and there's an empty seat right there, waiting to be filled!"

Maggie smiled. That was so typical of Mrs. Barker to worry about the one thing she had no control over. "Maybe it'll be filled after intermission," Maggie said, trying to cheer her up, but Mrs. Barker didn't hear. She was out of the pit as quickly as possible to check up on the things she did have control over, like the burned-out light in the lobby.

Maggie stood and stretched her legs then walked just outside the pit to wait for Mrs. Knightly to come. The people in the theatre were systematically filing out towards the concessions and restrooms, chattering one with another as they did. Maggie saw an arm wave at her from across the room and immediately recognized Selma moving aggressively through the crowd. She smiled and waved back, glad to be on the other side of the theatre.

"Maggie! Here we are!" Mrs. Knightly suddenly appeared next to Maggie. "Do you know Candy, the librarian from Trenton? No, you probably don't. She was hired after you left."

Maggie nodded towards Candy Turnbull, noticing her cool manner as she did. "Yes, I know Miss Turnbull," she said.

"Well, we met up before the play started and, seeing how we'd both come alone, decided to sit together. Of course, it took a bit of shuffling with a few agreeable people, but we finally managed to make it work in the end."

"I'm glad it turned out so well," Maggie offered. "So, what was it that you needed to talk to me about?"

"Yes, we should get right to the point, shouldn't we?" Mrs. Knightly said. "After all, there's not a lot of time left before act two begins, is there? The hospital papers you asked about, the day you came to visit—that's what I wanted to talk to you about."

Maggie was suddenly interested. "Have you found out anything about them?" she asked.

"No, actually. Just an empty folder in the mayor's filing cabinet. But that got me thinking. Perhaps you borrowed the papers for your young man—the one playing Scrooge tonight? Isn't he doing a fabulous job of it too, by the way. He really has the character down pat, I believe! But let's put that aside for now. Did you or he borrow the papers from the filing cabinet for his university project?"

Maggie was caught off guard by the assumption Mrs. Knightly had made. "No, neither of us borrowed them. I did, however, find some of the same papers in my husband's old files."

"You did? Where are they now?"

"Currently, they're on top of my piano, at my house."

"Oh. How unusual." Now it was Mrs. Knightly's turn to be caught off guard. "May I see them, perhaps tonight after the play? I'm just curious to know what's in them, especially since nobody seems to know anything about them."

"Of course. Do you know where I live?"

"With your mother, somewhere on Willow Drive?"

"Yes, I'm just a few blocks away, on the corner of Willow and Third—the house with the white shutters. I'll meet you there then, after the play?" Maggie smiled at Mrs. Knightly then turned to Miss Turnbull. "It was nice seeing you again."

"There are a lot of people from Trenton here tonight," Mrs. Knightly observed. "It was more than just luck that Candy and I found each other. And, look! Here's another one from our town, standing just behind you!"

Maggie turned as Mrs. Knightly greeted Nurse Kelli into the throng of fellow Trentonites. "You must've seen the flyers too, Kelli. Nice to see you here!"

Nurse Kelli seemed in a hurry but managed to smile at everyone as she passed by into the lobby.

"She's probably here with Jay Lindt from the city office," Mrs. Knightly said. "Dick Wood tells me they've been dating."

Hoping to avoid the gossip that was to follow about Nurse Kelli's dating situation, Maggie quickly made her excuses then ducked back into the orchestra pit. It was almost time for the entre'acte to begin anyway, and she didn't want to get the look again from Mrs. Barker.

CHAPTER TWENTY-FOUR

"I can't believe this! Now there's two seats vacant!"

Mrs. Barker couldn't seem to get her mind off the seating situation in the audience. As soon as the music for the entre'acte had ended, she was perched, once again, by the curtain and was peeking out at the vacant seats.

"That awful green coat is gone too!" she exclaimed. "At least I don't have to see that thing anymore!"

Maggie was amused by Mrs. Barker's obsession with the seats and noticed Dale Redding was smiling too, behind his drums. "She has a lot in common with my mom," he leaned over and whispered to Maggie.

Maggie nodded. She didn't even have to know Dale's mom to know what he was talking about. Maggie thought of her own Mother. She also could be very obsessive. Take, for instance, the hospital papers and her belief that they were connected to the mysterious deaths that had been happening, not to mention her unrealistic way of solving them—by making a list, of all things! Maggie never could see what good that would do. Even if she took the time to make a list, what would she put in it anyway? Mysterious papers?—that was a given. How about wool fibers under Coralee's nails and Dolores's flu shot? And, then there was the woman seen with Mayor Simple in the park who had on a green coat. Selma had mentioned that in the kitchen, the day of Dolores's funeral. She might as well add the dolphin pin she found in the library park to the list too. Why not? Her mother would put it there for sure! Maggie's mind was entertaining all these thoughts as she patiently waited for the next musical number to come. It surprised her when, suddenly and unexpectedly, she began to understand their relevance.

Green fibers under Coralee's nails...Dolores's flu shot... The dolphin pin... A woman in a green coat... A green coat!!!

"What did you say?" Mrs. Barker asked Maggie. "Something about that horrid green coat?"

Maggie hadn't meant to say that last thought aloud. "I think I need some air," she said, suddenly standing. Her heart was beating so fast, she thought it would burst through her chest any minute.

"Yes, I think you do," Mrs. Barker agreed. "You've gone a funny color, you know."

Maggie didn't respond. She quickly slipped out of the orchestra pit and hurried through the lobby and out the door, keenly aware she might already be too late. Running as fast as she could, she made her way down the snowy sidewalk, hoping and praying she'd get there in time.

When she got closer to home, she could see the familiar light coming from the parlor window ahead. Her eyes strained to make out any figures inside. The sidewalk was icy, and she started to slip then quickly steadied herself. It wouldn't do to fall right now—she needed to pay more attention to where she was going, so she wouldn't injure herself. It wouldn't do for her to be lying helpless on the sidewalk, not with the danger that lay ahead. Carefully, she stepped across the ice, only to find herself slipping again. Suddenly, she heard her name shouted out. It startled her enough to make her loose her balance entirely. This time she went down, landing upon the snowy sidewalk below.

"Mrs. Brown!"

Someone was running towards her. She looked up, frantically trying to see who it was. In the glare of the streetlight, she was surprised to see the dark figure of Zachy standing over her, trying to help her up.

"You're not hurt, are you?" he asked, concerned.

"Zachy! Listen to me carefully!" Maggie quickly got on her feet then grabbed him by the shoulders to get his full attention. "You've got to run to your house as quickly as possible and call the police. Do you understand? There's an intruder inside my house! Tell the police to come right away!"

"An intruder? Are you sure it's…"

"Zachy!" Maggie shouted at him. "Do it now! There's no time for questions!"

Zachy looked at her, alarmed by the intense look on her face, then ran off as fast as he could go. Maggie crossed the street to her own house. Soon, she was bursting through the front door, ready to confront a murderer.

CHAPTER TWENTY-FIVE

"Maggie, you're here."

Her mom was standing next to Kelli Sanderson, unaware of the danger she was in. "Why are you here? Is the play over already?"

"No, Mom. I knew someone was planning on coming tonight to see you—so I came as quickly as I could. This is Nurse Kelli, from Trenton. She's interested in our hospital papers."

"Yes, she told me. That's okay, isn't it? Is something wrong?"

Kelli gave a short laugh. "Of course, it's okay. Just hand them to me, now!" She held out her hand for the folder.

Maggie's mother looked at her, confused. "Maggie, what exactly is happening?"

"Just hand her the papers, Mom, and she'll be on her way."

Suddenly, Nurse Kelli grabbed Maggie's mom by her arm and pulled her into the middle of the room with one hand. Maggie saw the syringe in her other hand.

"You don't have to do that," Maggie said. "You can take the papers and go, and we'll forget all about this. He isn't worth it."

"How do you know if he's worth it or not? You know nothing of what I've had to do for him!" Nurse Kelli shouted back.

"You had to clear the way for him, didn't you? You loved him and wanted it all to work out so you had to kill the one person who knew about it. It was the only way you could get the money from the hospital fund—if Mayor Simple was out of the picture."

"Mayor Simple just wouldn't let it go. He knew too much. I needed to do it, Maggie. I had no
other choice. It was so easy, you see. He was always in the library park at noon, and I had my bag with me... so easy."

"And what about Dolores? That must've been easy too, giving her the flu shot at the city offices the day she died. What could be easier?"

"I just wanted to give her a scare, that was all. How did I know she was going to drive off that bridge!? You've got to believe me! Dolores's death was an accident! She shouldn't have been driving at all after what I gave her."

"Okay, accident or not, you had them out of your way now. I understand. But what about Coralee, the mayor's sister? How was she in your way?"

"Another accident—not my fault! That girl from Selma's Real Estate gave me her address and told me she had the desk —the desk that had the papers in it—or, at least, I *thought* it did. I didn't know until tonight that they'd been here at your house all along!"

"So, you broke into Coralee's apartment to get them?"

"No, I didn't break in—her door was unlocked. I saw her leave, so I went in to find the papers. How was I to know she'd come right back? That crazy woman came at me, screaming, so I pushed her. She fell back, hitting her head on the desk. I tried to help her—I always carry my bag, you see. I put my surgical gloves on and took her pulse first, ready to do whatever was needed. But she was past helping."

"So, that wasn't your fault either," Maggie said, trying to keep Kelli talking in hopes that the police would hurry and get there. She knew she needed to find a way to get that syringe out of her hands too. No telling what deadly concoction she had in it.

"No, it wasn't my fault! I had no problem with Coralee Simple. How in the world would I know she'd come at me like that? I had to defend myself!"

"I understand why you had to do what you did. There were obstacles and you and to remove them. But my mom won't try to stop you—I won't either, Kelli. Just take the papers and go. There's no reason to do what you're planning on doing."

Nurse Kelli slowly began to lower the syringe, ready to give in. Suddenly, in the still of the moment, a soft meow was heard from above. Maggie looked up. Candy Corn had somehow gotten in the house and was standing next to Zachy, of all people! He was standing in the loft, holding his net high above his head, ready to toss it.

"No, Zachy, No!" Maggie shouted.

She watched, horrified, as Zachy threw the net. Maggie quickly jumped forward and pulled her mom out of the way just as the net came down upon Nurse Kelli, who immediately fell to the floor under its weight. She twisted and turned every which way, trying to free herself. The syringe fell out of her hand and rolled away, just out of reach.

Suddenly, the front door flew open and Detective Milton rushed into the room with Russ Secrist at his side.

"You'll want to bag that," he said, pointing to the syringe. He looked at Maggie. "I thought the music was a bit thin on the second act," he said, smiling.

Maggie looked helplessly at her mother, not sure whether to laugh or cry.

"What was confusing was those darn hospital papers!"

Detective Milton was sitting in the parlor, talking to Maggie. A patrol car had taken Kelli Sanderson away. Jay Lindt was already behind bars, arrested by Russ Secrist that very night at the airport as he tried to escape with embezzled city funds. Dick Wood, Trenton's city manager, had alerted the police of his flight. He'd also provided evidence that was needed for Jay's arrest.

"You see, everyone involved knew Mayor Simple had some papers in his possession, papers he considered valuable. But the hospital minutes you gave me months ago had no real value —seemingly. They had a lot of value to Jay though. They were proof of a great deal of money that had been hidden for decades and easy, therefore, to embezzle. As city clerk, he was in position to move the funds around to his advantage after he'd found out about them. He put them into a bond first, then when that matured, he switched them to his own bank account. All in all, it has taken him a year to finally work out all the details. He only knew about the hidden account in the first place because of an article your husband was working on. He was interviewing someone from a nursing home, I believe."

"Yes," Maggie replied. "Mr. Clyde Haswell."

"Yes, he's the one. Well, apparently, at that time, your husband went to the city offices and asked Jay to find out what he knew about the claim Mr. Haswell was making—about the large amount of money he'd contributed to the hospital fund. When Jay checked into it—well, that's when he discovered the account that had been forgotten. When he casually mentioned it to Kelli Sanderson, she took it upon herself to systematically remove any obstacles that stood in the way."

"But the murders? Surely, Jay wasn't involved in them—or was he?"

"He's pleading innocent to the murders. He claims he had no idea, until just recently, that Kelli was 'clearing the way' for him. He thought the deaths that were happening were just fortunate outcomes—fortunate, that is, for him. They left him as the sole person who had knowledge of the lost funds, making it easier for him to embezzle them. Of course, our investigation is still underway, but it's looking like the murders were all Kelli Sanderson's work."

"I still can't believe Nurse Kelli could do such a thing."

"Love is a powerful motive, and money even more. The hospital committee raised over half a million dollars. Now, that's a powerful motive, if you ask me. If it hadn't been for you— going to the Simples' house that day and finding those minutes—well, Jay Lindt and Kelli Sanderson both might have gotten away with their crimes."

"Glad I was able to help," Maggie replied, her heart not really in it.

Detective Milton suddenly and uncharacteristically began to squirm in his seat. "There's one thing more, Maggie, that you need to know." He nervously began to clear his throat.

Maggie looked at him, waiting. She noticed his demeanor had suddenly changed. He was looking down at his big, rough hands, as if the words he needed to say were written on them. Finally, he looked up at her.

"Jay has been doing a lot of confessing since we brought him in. Apparently, he and Kelli had a big fight, and in her anger, she told him everything she'd done—all the obstacles she'd removed for him. Well, the first obstacle, you see, was…"

He paused, looking at his hands again. He hated this part of his job. After all these years on the force, he still had a hard time doing it.

Suddenly, the dolphin pin popped back into Maggie's mind and she knew at once what Detective Milton was trying to tell her. It had been pinned on Nurse Kelli's white uniform the night Wesley had been born.

"The first obstacle was Hal," Maggie said, feeling like the wind had just been knocked out of her. "That night at the hospital, he really didn't have to die, did he?" She looked at Detective Milton, waiting for an answer.

"No, Maggie. I'm sorry. There's every chance he would have lived, even with his injuries. When he came in that night to the emergency room, an opportunity presented itself to Sanderson, and she took it. She shouldn't have even been working in the emergency room at all, but because of the storm, all hospital personnel were working double shifts and were moved around as needed. I'm so sorry, Maggie."

Maggie remained seated, silently watching the expression of sorrow on Detective Milton's face. She felt like time had stopped for her and would never start again unless she made the first step. Slowly, she tried to stand, only to find herself collapsing into Detective Milton's capable hands.

CHAPTER TWENTY-SIX

There were only two days left before Christmas, and Maggie and her kids were in the kitchen with Grandma, putting together Christmas plates for their neighbors and friends. The air was full of the sweet aroma of sugar and vanilla. Grandma and the girls were singing carols and Wesley sat in his highchair, sampling some of the goodies. Christmas was right around the corner and all moods were, seemingly, cheerful and bright. All, that is, except Maggie's.

Grief had found its way inside her heart once again. The news Detective Milton had given her had caused a big setback and Maggie found herself reliving Hal's death as if it had happened just yesterday instead of a year ago. She tried to hide it—she didn't want to ruin Christmas for the kids—but was finding it hard to do.

She knew the only thing for it was to keep things as normal as possible. She was grateful for the holiday traditions that kept her moving from day to day and from one project to another. She tried not to look too far ahead, knowing one step at a time was all she could manage for now. *When the holidays were over, perhaps my grief will end too,* she thought. If not, she wasn't sure what she'd do.

Soon the plates were all wrapped up in festive red bows and ready for delivery. The first ones were for Zachy and his family and then for Sophie across the street. Maggie let Susan and Janie carry the plates up to each porch and ring the bell.

"Merry Christmas!" they shouted as the plates were delivered.

The next stop was Mrs. Barker's house. Maggie listened to her tell how much she'd appreciated her playing the piano for the play and hoped she'd be available for the next one, come February.

"We'll be doing *Guys and Dolls*. It's a classic! You'll really love the music too. And Rob Stanger has already said he'd play Sky Masterson. You've really got to be part of it!"

Maggie smiled but made no promises.

Benson's house was next, and then Dale Redding's. Maggie had a lengthy discussion with Dale on his front porch.

"All the facts are there," she told him as she handed Hal's folders to him. "You can pick up where he left off, if you'd like to look them over."

"You know I would, Maggie. And I'll see to it that the hospital money gets used somehow, for what it was originally intended. The power of the press can get things done, as you well know. Perhaps the money can go towards the new cancer addition."

"And the plaques? Will you make sure they have a prominent place in the foyer of the new addition, to thank those who donated so much so long ago?"

Dale assured her that he'd take care of it all.

Next, the girls took turns giving plates to their teachers. First, the school teachers, and then the Sunday School teacher. When that was accomplished, it was Maggie's turn to take a plate to her piano students who lived in town. As quick as she tried to be, there was always a parent or two who'd get into a long conversation about their children's musical progress. It was late in the afternoon by the time they were through delivering all the plates.

"There's one more I'd like to deliver," Maggie told her mom when they got home. "If you'll watch the kids for me for a few hours, I'd like to take a plate to Mr. Haswell at the nursing home."

"No problem," her mother told her. "Me and the kids will watch *Frosty the Snowman* while you're gone. It's on tonight, you know."

Maggie hugged her mom and thought, for the millionth time, how she would ever manage without her.

After the long commute, she was led into Mr. Haswell's room by a very cheerful nurse.

"You have a visitor," she chirped. "I'll be back in a bit to take you down to the rec-room." She turned to Maggie to explain. "It's our annual Christmas party tonight—dinner then a program provided by community artists. We have a choral group and a string ensemble, then a reading of 'The Night Before Christmas' from a local radio personality. It's going to be a fun evening for our residents." She smiled at Mr. Haswell then left, humming under her breath.

"Mr. Haswell, do you remember me?" Maggie asked as she sat down in the chair in front of him. He was sitting in his usual overstuffed chair and was all dressed up in a suit and tie, ready for the party.

"You know, I can't have any of those cookies you brought," he told her, disgustedly. "Diabetes. Had it for years."

"Oh, I'm sorry. I didn't know."

"No, you wouldn't have, would you? Are you the lady who came before, asking about the hospital? Have you come to tell me about the plaque? Did they get it up yet, there in the lobby?"

"Not yet, but your plaque will be going up soon, probably by spring, I would guess."

"Well, it certainly took them long enough," Mr. Haswell said in his usual complaining way.

"And in a few days' time, you'll be getting another visitor. reporter—Dale Redding. He's coming to do an article about you in his newspaper."

"I've already had a reporter interview me and nothing came of it. First, they forgot to put up the plaque, then they forgot to put my interview in the paper. I looked for it for a long time, but it wasn't there! What's wrong with people now-a-days? Why don't they finish what they start?"

"Mr. Redding will finish your interview," Maggie assured him. "The other reporter—the one from a year ago—well, he was my husband. He wanted to finish the article for you, it just wasn't possible for him to do so."

Mr. Haswell looked skeptical. "Something better came up did it? Something more interesting? Or did he just lose interest in the story? Perhaps he didn't finish it because it got too costly, traveling back and forth to interview me. If it was a matter of cost, why didn't the newspaper step in and give him an allowance for travel? Really, sometimes employers can be so cheap!"

Suddenly, he noticed Maggie's distress. He hadn't meant to make her feel bad—he just couldn't help but complain—had done it for years. "Was it the cost?" he asked, trying to be sympathetic. "Was the cost too much to pay?"

Maggie tried to hold back the tears. "You have no idea," she said.

CHAPTER TWENTY-SEVEN

Christmas Day had finally come and so had Santa Claus. Janie got a shiny new bike and some clothes for her Barbie, Susan got the Strawberry Shortcake Doll she'd asked for, and Wesley got a Radio Flyer filled with his favorite snacks. The smell of homemade rolls and a turkey baking permeated the house, reminding Maggie of past Christmases when she was just a young girl herself. She remembered how thrilled she'd been to find a Saucy Walker doll under the tree one Christmas— something that she'd been wanting for a long time. She had gotten up in the middle of the night to peek through the railing to see if Santa had really left it. There it was, under the tree, waiting for her. Excited, she'd fallen asleep in the loft that night and had to be carried back to bed by her father.

After dinner was over, they all got another surprise when Dillon, Sharlene and the boys showed up unexpectedly.

"It was a last-minute thing," Dillon explained to Maggie and their Mom, "so instead of calling first, we thought we'd surprise you!"

Maggie's mother gave them all a hug. "This is the best surprise ever! Christmas day with both of my children, and all five of my grandchildren! Who could ask for more?"

Sam and Kenny ran off to find the girls to see what Santa had brought them.

"If we'd known you'd be here, we would've waited on dinner," Maggie said as she took their coats. "We've already eaten!"

"You know my favorites are the left-overs, Maggie. How about a turkey sandwich with some of Mom's cranberry sauce?"

"And I'll take some pie, if there's any left," Sharlene added. "Banana Cream."

"How long can you stay this time?" Maggie asked.

"Sharlene needs to be back to the office by Monday morning."

"Oh, that's too bad. But I'm glad you're here, even if it is for only a few days."

Sharlene sat at the table, ready to have her pie. "My boss paid for the plane tickets for us to come, you see, so we couldn't turn down his offer," she explained. "He wants me to hand deliver a check for a client who lives in Trenton, so I arranged to do it all over Christmas so we could spend the holiday together."

"Trenton, huh?" Maggie was interested. "Who's your client, or is that confidential?"

"No, no—there's no secret there. Let's see." She pulled an envelope from her purse and read the name written across it. "Trenton City Library, care of Miss Candy Turnbull. It seems the mayor of Trenton had arranged with my boss to have an original Mark Twain manuscript auctioned off with us, with instructions that the proceeds be donated to the Trenton City Library.

But, before he could get the manuscript to us, well—he died. So, we thought, that was that. But then, lo and behold, his solicitor—a Mr. Graves—brought it to us months later with the instructions to proceed as originally planned. But I must be boring you with all these details!

How have you been, Maggie? Was that play of yours a success?"

Maggie couldn't sleep that night. She kept tossing and turning as her mind replayed the details of the past week. So, there had been two different sets of papers—one containing the hospital minutes and the other the Mark Twain Manuscript. She wondered which one she'd been meant to find and realized the outcome would have been entirely different had she found the Mark Twain papers instead. It all made sense to her now, why Brad Bennington had wanted to find them so badly and why he'd hired Rob to look for them. Her mind kept looping over the different scenarios. At least Candy Turnbull would get her library addition now, with or without the city council's approval. That was one good thing in the whole awful mess.

She got out of bed after a while and pulled on her Levi's and sweatshirt then slipped on her shoes. Perhaps, a short walk would help clear her head. She stopped in the kitchen for a drink of water first. *If only Hal was still here,* she thought for the millionth time, she could talk to him. She could tell him about the papers she'd found and about the murders that had been committed because of them. Then he'd say something profound and she would unburden all her thoughts on him. He would, bit by bit, help her sort everything out. but he wasn't here and she knew, sadly, that he wasn't coming back. It was time to move on. Nothing good could come of her wishing any different.

Maggie heard a faint knock coming from the back door. It made her jump slightly. She cautiously walked over and peeked out, then opened the door wide.

"What in the world are you doing here this time of night!?" she demanded. "Do you have any idea what time it is!?"

Rob Stanger stood on the back porch, looking a bit sheepish. "Sorry, I wouldn't have dared to bother you except, well, I saw your lights on as I drove by, so I thought I'd stop and see if you were still up and if you wanted to come with me on an assignment. I really think you'll be interested in coming, considering your personal involvement in the matter." He stepped into the kitchen, hesitantly.

Maggie looked at him, not believing his excuse for one minute. "You can't be serious! At this time of night!? Why would you think I'd want to go on an assignment with you in the middle of the night?" She turned away from him briefly, wishing that things were different, that she was different. Why couldn't he accept that she needed more time? Suddenly, she turned back and glared at him. "Who sends you on an assignment this late anyway?"

"Wow, Maggie. You ask a lot of questions. Actually, I've been hired by Mrs. Knightly."

"Sorry if I don't believe you," Maggie said accusingly. "Why in the world would she hire you? Are you on a stake-out or something? Is that why you're working this late at night?"

"Again, with the questions! Just say you'll come with me and I'll explain the rest on the way. How about it?" He looked at her hopefully.

"I'm not coming with you on a stake out or anything else for that matter, especially not this late. Who does she have you spying on? Does she want you to dig up some dirt on Trenton's new mayor? Find out what he's really like?"

"It's not a stake out," Rob said defensively. "And she hasn't hired me to spy on anybody either. Mrs. Knightly has hired me to—well… to *adjust* the siren behind Trenton City Offices. She knows it's the only way they'll get rid of it if somehow, mysteriously, it gets—broken."

Maggie stared at him, speechless. He stared back, waiting for a reaction—any reaction—but Maggie seemed frozen in place.

Then slowly, from the corners of her mouth, a smile began to form. Soon, it had spread across her entire face, giving Rob hope. "You'll come then?" he asked.

Maggie turned suddenly and ran out of the kitchen, leaving him alone. Rob shrugged. He hadn't expected this reaction from her. "Wait…" he called after her, feeling defeated. "Won't you reconsider? I didn't mean to…"

Maggie suddenly appeared again. "I was just getting my coat," she said matter-of-factly, putting it on as she hurried outside. "C'mon, there's no time to waste! That siren has needed *adjusting* for a long time!"

Smiling, Rob quickly followed her out the door.

ABOUT THE AUTHOR

 Ann Buys is a musician and composer with numerous published compositions to her name. An avid reader of cozy mysteries, she enjoys the process of writing them as well. THE PAPER TRAIL MYSTERY is the first book in the *Piano Teacher Mysteries,* a series she created featuring amateur sleuth Maggie Brown. Ann also writes books for middle grade readers and has one published in this genre. When not writing, she loves playing the piano, sitting in her favorite comfy chair with a cozy mystery, and spending time with family and friends.